Miss Cute Candy was eyeing Bonny up and down.

'Where's all your stuff?'

'I haven't got any.'

'What, none? No make-up? Nothing for your nails? No stuff to fix your hair?'

Poor Bonny's heart was sinking. 'No. None of that.'

'I don't see why you're even here,' said Miss Cute Candy. 'What's the point of showing up if all you're going to be is One Big Nothing?'

Forced to spend a day at Charm School while her mother is on a course, Bonny makes some surprising – and hilarious – discoveries . . .

Also available by Anne Fine,
and published by Corgi Yearling

BAD DREAMS

www.annefine.co.uk

For Susanna,

Charm School

with love, ~~Anne Fine~~

Anne Fine

Illustrated by Ros Asquith

CORGI YEARLING BOOKS

CHARM SCHOOL
A CORGI YEARLING BOOK: 0 440 86400 3

First published in Great Britain by Doubleday,
a division of Transworld Publishers

PRINTING HISTORY
Doubleday edition published 1999
Corgi Yearling edition published 2000

13 15 17 19 20 18 16 14 12

Acknowledgement is made of the quotations from 'She Walks in
Beauty' by Lord Byron (1815) on p. 95 and 'Ode on A Grecian Urn' by
John Keats (1820) on p. 179.

Corgi Yearling Books are published by Transworld Publishers,
61-63 Uxbridge Road, Ealing, London W5 5SA,
a division of The Random House Group Ltd,
in Australia by Random House Australia Pty Ltd,
20 Alfred Street, Milsons Point, NSW 2061, Australia,
in New Zealand by Random House New Zealand,
18 Poland Road, Glenfield, Auckland, New Zealand
and in South Africa by Random House (Pty) Ltd,
Endulini, 5a Jubilee Road, Parktown 2193, South Africa.

Made and printed in Great Britain by
Cox & Wyman Ltd, Reading, Berks

CHAPTER ONE

'I can't choose anything,' wailed Bonny, tossing the brochure on the floor. 'Not out of this horrible lot. Why can't I just stay here?'

'Oh, yes,' scoffed her mother. 'Spend the whole day alone here, in a house where the furniture hasn't even arrived yet. Next door to people we haven't even met, who might be axe-murderers. Oh, yes!' She picked up the brochure. 'Now, quickly, sweetheart. Choose one of the classes, or I'll have to choose one for you.'

Bonny snatched the brochure and went down the list again. 'Copperplate Handwriting!' she groaned. 'Practical Parenting! Defensive Driving! And Charm School!' She hurled it back down. 'All right, all right! I've chosen. I'll do Practical Parenting.'

'You can't do that. It says you need a baby.'

'I'll borrow one.'

'Don't be silly. You haven't even met anyone your own age yet. How could you find a *baby*?' Her mother glanced impatiently at her watch. 'Now listen, Bonny. We haven't time for any more of this. We have to leave now. This new job's important to me. I only have one day to brush up my accounting skills and pass the test to get my certificate. And my class starts at nine. So choose now. *Choose*.'

Bonny scowled horribly. The packing. The move. Losing her friends. A whole empty summer yawning in front of her, with absolutely no company, before starting again in a strange school. She was as miserable as she could be.

'Why can't I just come with you?'

'What? To Bookkeeping (Advanced)? You don't know anything at all about bookkeeping.'

It sounded so babyish to say, 'The way I feel, I'd rather just sit next to you all day, not understanding anything, than be sent off to do something of my own.' Instead, Bonny said sullenly:

'So? I don't even know what copperplate handwriting is, I'm too young to drive, and I may never have a baby.'

Her mother laughed and reached for the car keys. 'You know what this means, don't you, Bonbons?'

'No,' said Bonny. 'No, no, no.' She kicked out at the bright pink sheet of paper that had fallen from the brochure.

'No!' she said again. 'I am not going to Charm School.'

'Get in the car.'

'No,' said Bonny. 'Not if you paid me forty million pounds. Not if you boiled me in oil. Not if you begged me with tears rolling down your cheeks like pearls.'

'Get in the car.'

'If you do this to me,' Bonny warned her mother, 'I'll never speak to you again. I won't take out the rubbish. I won't make you pots of tea when you're tired. I won't bring home any of the notes from school. And I'll grow up to be a round-the-world yachtswoman, so you won't just have to worry about me for a few hours now and then. You'll have to worry about me *day* and *night.*'

'Charming!' said Mrs Bramble.

'See?' Bonny said desperately. 'I am already charming. I don't *need* lessons in it.'

Mrs Bramble glanced at her watch for the last time. 'This discussion is over,' she warned. 'I have a job to keep, so get in the car and sit on it quietly before I smack it!'

The woman behind the desk peered doubtfully at Bonny's scowl and Bonny's faded jeans.

'Charm School? Are you sure? To me, she looks a little more like Woodwork I, or Starting French.'

'French only lasts an hour,' said Mrs Bramble. 'And Woodwork I doesn't begin till tomorrow. It's all today we need.'

Seeing the puzzled look on the woman's

face, she went on to explain.

'You see, I'm just starting a new job and I need to learn better accounting skills. And her father's still sitting in a lay-by with a broken down furniture van. And obviously she hasn't had any time to make any new friends yet—'

'I don't want new friends,' Bonny interrupted sourly. 'I want my old friends back.'

Mrs Bramble bit her lip, then bravely carried on. 'And what with the telephone not working yet, it wasn't possible to find a sitter. So ...'

She peered anxiously at her daughter, who glared back in a mixture of irritation and humiliation.

'Still ...' the woman said, still doubtful. '*Charm* School ...?'

'That's all there is,' said Mrs Bramble. 'Apart from Copperplate Handwriting. Unless you let her off the baby ...'

'Oh, no,' the woman said. 'You can't do Practical Parenting without a baby. You have to bathe it, you see.' She gave Bonny a nervous glance, as if she feared someone who looked as sullen and resentful as Mrs Bramble's daughter would just as soon drown a baby as wash it nicely behind the ears. 'One all-day Charm School it is, then,' she said, taking the money. 'And one all-day Bookkeeping (Advanced).'

She handed over the tickets. 'You'd better hurry,' she warned Mrs Bramble. 'Bookkeeping always starts dead on time. Don't worry about your daughter. I'll point her in the right direction.'

Mrs Bramble pecked Bonny hastily on the cheek. 'Bye, sweetheart. See you later.'

And she fled.

The woman ushered Bonny into the lift. 'You might as well take it,' she said. 'Even though you're not carrying any of the usual stuff.'

'The usual stuff?'

But just at that moment the lift doors closed, and Bonny found she was talking to herself.

Bonny got out of the lift on the third floor, as she'd been told, and stamped her foot.

'Horrible!' she muttered. 'Horrible, horrible, horrible! I hate this town. I hate this place. I hate the world. I hate everybody!'

'Wrong floor, I think,' a voice beside her said.

Bonny spun round and told the man hurrying round the corner into the lift, 'This is three, isn't it? Where I'm supposed to be?'

He looked her up and down. 'I don't think so, Little Miss Grumpy. Unless, of course, you're here to help Maura with the sound and the lighting. The only other people on this floor today are Mrs Opalene's pupils.'

'That's right,' Bonny said stubbornly. 'And I'm one of them.'

'Oh, yes?' As if to show how little he believed her, he put his foot in the lift doorway to stop it closing. 'So where's all your stuff?'

A tinned voice spurted out of the lift ceiling. *'Please check the doors for obstructions.'*

Startled, the man drew back his foot. The lift doors closed.

Fed up with people as good as telling her to her face that she was a Charm-free Zone, Bonny seized the opportunity to stick out her tongue, dig her thumbs in her ears, and waggle her fingers.

The lift doors opened again, and the man stared.

'I was quite wrong,' he said before they slid closed again properly. 'You were quite right. This is quite obviously the floor you need.'

All along the corridor were photographs of dolls. All sorts of dolls, from innocent blue-eyed china dolls to mischievous dark-eyed dolls. But all had shiny eyes with curly lashes, and clouds of perfect hair, and pearly teeth behind their painted, triumphant smiles. They all had names as well, printed beneath their pictures. Miss Rosebud, one was called. Miss Sweet Caroline was another. Little Miss Cute Candy hung between Princess Royale and Our Million Dollar Baby. And Miss Stardust even had a wand to match her glittery frock.

Miss Treasure   Miss Rosebud

Along the corridor came the tea boy, pushing his trolley. 'Are you lost?' he asked Bonny.

'No. I just stopped to look.'

'Choosing your favourite?'

Bonny stared at him coolly. 'I don't think so. I'm a bit old for dollies.'

The tea boy nodded at the pictures. 'Never too old to look like a twink.'

Bonny took a closer look at Miss Cute Candy. 'Are you *serious*? Are you telling me she's *real*?'

'*Real*?' said the tea boy. 'She's a tiger, that one. She just this minute bit my head off for running a trolley wheel over one of her diamanté shoes.'

'What's diamanté?'

'Don't ask me,' he shrugged. 'That's what she called it when she threw her little tantrum.'

'Where is she now?' asked Bonny, a little nervously.

'Where do you think?' said the tea boy. 'She's behind that door with the others, spending the day in Charm School.'

Bonny was horrified. 'It didn't say!' she wailed. 'It didn't say anything on the pink sheet about dressing up like dollies!'

The tea boy shrugged. 'So? It doesn't say anything on the Woodwork I sheet about needing sticking plasters. Or on the Practical Parenting sheet about bringing your aspirins.'

'It's going to be *awful*, isn't it?' Bonny said.

'It's going to be *worse* than awful,' said the tea boy. 'It's always awful. But usually on Saturdays it's just Mrs Opalene's Charm School girls. They're bad enough. But on the one day a year she does the Curls and Purls

Show, we get a flood of dippy twinks from The Little Miss Pretty Circle. So it's *worse.*'

'The Little Miss Pretty Circle?' (It didn't just sound *worse.* It sounded *frightful.*)

He nodded at the photos on the walls. 'You'll see,' he warned her. 'Just go in and see.'

Bonny pushed open the door, and peeped inside. A dozen girls her age were sitting on chairs facing a little stage. Their backs were straight. Their hands were folded in their laps. And they were listening.

Up on the stage, a large, round, glittering lady strolled up and down.

'You're all *Stars*,' she was telling them. 'Every one of you. But when you come up on this stage, you're going to be *Superstars*!'

Bonny slid in the room and closed the door behind her. Nobody turned to look.

'All day I want to see your Prettiest Eyes and your Prettiest Smiles!'

Bonny took a seat on a chair in the back row, and nobody noticed.

'All day,' said the glittering lady, 'I shall be watching you. And do you know what I'm expecting to see?'

'Yes, Mrs Opalene,' chirruped a dozen little voices, quite drowning out Bonny's baffled, 'No.'

'I am expecting to see you walk as if you were on the brink of dancing.'

'Yes, Mrs Opalene.'

Mrs Opalene lifted a hand to her ear. 'And all day long I shall be listening. And do you know what I'm expecting to hear?'

'Yes, Mrs Opalene,' chirruped everyone except Bonny.

'I am expecting to hear you all talking as if you were about to burst into song.'

'Yes, Mrs Opalene.' Nobody sniggered. Nobody made a face. Nobody even turned to look at the person next to them.

'And when you're singing,' said Mrs Opalene. 'What am I expecting?'

'To hear an angel trying to get it absolutely right,' came the reply.

'And when you dance?'

'To be dazzled by our delicate footwork.'

'That's right. Lovely!' She clapped her hands together. Her rings flashed. 'So now we'll just go ahead and do everything we usually do on Saturday mornings in Charm School. But in the afternoon we'll have our special Curls and Purls Show.' Her eyes shone with excitement. 'And, just before you go home, we'll have The Crowning of The Supreme Queen, who gets to choose her very own pretty name to wear all year. And haven't we had some lovely ones!' She pressed her hands together, remembering. 'Miss Perfect Pearl! Miss Treasure! Dazzling Miss Daisy! Miss Sparkling Sue ...'

All round, everyone was clapping delightedly, except for Bonny, who sat with her head in her hands, even more sure now that she was in the wrong place, at the wrong time, with the wrong people. Should she get up and run? But there was something about the rising chatter round her, like sparrows squabbling on a fence, that made her feel even more homesick for her old friends.

So she'd give it a go. Someone would have to speak to her some time, after all. And maybe, even in this unlikely cluster of goody-two-shoes, she might find some company to keep her going through the long, lonely summer, till she could make some proper, sensible friends in her new school.

So when Mrs Opalene told everyone to take a little break while she set out her table for Beauty Tips, Bonny looked up. And when a girl she recognized from the photographs on the wall outside sailed past her, flashing a sparkling smile, Bonny said to her hopefully, 'Hello, Rosebud.'

The pretty vision twirled around. 'Who said that?'

'I did.'

'Why?'

Bonny stared. 'Because I don't know anyone here,' she said. 'And you just smiled at me.'

'I didn't smile at you,' the pretty vision snapped. 'I was just practising being *charming*.'

And off she went.

Rude, horrid *baggage*, thought Bonny. But it didn't seem fair to judge the whole lot of them by one bad-mannered, haughty girl. So when the one that Bonny recognized as Miss Sweet Caroline strolled over towards her, smiling, Bonny tried again.

'Hi, Caroline.'

The smile vanished instantly. The eyes flashed sparks of fire. And Miss Sweet Caroline said to Bonny, 'You say that again, and I'll stick your head in a holly bush.'

She swung on the heel of her shiny satin shoe, and stalked off, scowling. Bonny stared after her, astonished, until another of the girls came up behind. Though her hair was even longer and glossier than on the photograph outside, Bonny could tell it was Miss Stardust.

'Brilliant!' she said to Bonny. 'You certainly showed her!'

Bonny was baffled. All that she'd done to Miss Sweet Caroline was say hello.

'Showed who?' she asked.

'Silly old Sarajane.' Miss Stardust nodded after Miss Sweet Caroline. 'That was a smart way to remind her of the last time she won anything – about a million years ago! And she certainly needn't expect to win the glistering tiara today.'

'What glistering tiara?'

Miss Stardust waggled her pretty head from side to side in impatience.

'Why, the glistering tiara of Miss Supreme Queen, of course. Weren't you even *listening*?'

Suddenly Bonny couldn't even see her. A cloud of candy-floss hair had stepped between them. 'You can't be *Miss* Supreme Queen,' it corrected Miss Stardust officiously. 'You'd have to be "Your Highness, The Supreme Queen".'

'Well, thank you so very much, Cristalle,' snarled Miss Stardust. 'For wasting a whole corner of my brain by filling it up with something I don't need to know.'

'No,' snapped back Cristalle. 'I suppose you don't, Angelica, since you have absolutely no chance of winning it.'

Like Sarajane, she stalked off, just in time to pretend not to have heard Miss Stardust's cross-patchy hiss of, 'Neither have you!'

Bonny stared. Were they *all* horrid? Why had she thought they were like sparrows squabbling merrily on a fence? These girls were more like vultures, all hovering unpleasantly over the next glistering tiara to be won.

'Tell me,' she said to Angelica. 'Do you only get a photo on the wall outside if you're the winner?'

'That's right.'

'And, if you lose, do you have to wait a whole year to try again?'

'Yes,' said Angelica. 'And, if you win, you're crowned for the whole year.' Coughing politely, she modestly inspected her perfect finger-nails.

Bonny took the hint.

'So are you still Miss Stardust?'

'Yes, I am,' said Angelica firmly. 'I am Miss Stardust until four o'clock this afternoon. That gives me six hours, three minutes and—' She glanced at her watch. 'Fifteen seconds.'

Either she was a whizz at maths, thought Bonny, or she kept track by the second. Still trying to be friendly, she said to Angelica, 'But you might win again.'

Somehow, Angelica suddenly looked horribly anxious, and Bonny found herself adding hastily, in order to comfort her, 'Not that it matters. After all, winning isn't all that important.'

Angelica gasped. Her mouth dropped open and her eyes travelled up and down Bonny as if she were inspecting her properly for the first time: hair, face and clothing. She looked confused. 'Why are you here anyway?' she asked curiously after a moment. 'You've never come before. And look at you! You obviously haven't fallen to earth from Planet Fashion.'

Bonny couldn't help staring. If one of her old friends had said something like that, she would have thought that they were trying to be horrible. After all, it was the rudest thing that anyone had said to her in quite a while. But Miss Stardust somehow said it as if she were making a simple judgement of the facts, like 'Your eyes are more blue than green', or, 'It's really too wet for a picnic.'

And it was the truth. No way round that. There's nothing amazing about a pair of blue jeans and a faded shirt, and plain blue canvas sneakers. So Bonny was about to explain about her mother and the bookkeeping, and Dad stuck in the lay-by, and being new in town, when up sailed Miss Cute Candy, walking for all the world as if she were on the brink of dancing, pointing her pretty, sparkling shoes like a ballerina fairy, and waving her fingers elegantly in the air, as if the polish on her nails were still not dry.

'Who's this?' she demanded of Angelica, staring at Bonny.

'How should I know?' Angelica responded petulantly. 'I only just met her.' She turned away, making it clear that the last thing she wanted was to be caught up in conversation with Miss Cute Candy. Why were they all so scratchy with one another, Bonny wondered. And then she realized. If the whole day was a sort of competition, and they were rivals, then each time they even looked at one another, all they would see would be one more person who might snatch away that delectable, desirable, glistering tiara. What tiny-minded *pains* they were clearly going to be, even for a few short hours.

Now Miss Cute Candy was eyeing Bonny up and down.

'Where's all your stuff?'

'I haven't got any.'

'What, none? No make-up? Nothing for your nails? No stuff to fix your hair?'

Poor Bonny's heart was sinking. 'No. None of that.'

'Well, what about music tapes for your routine, and instructions for the lighting?'

'I haven't got those, either.'

Miss Cute Candy stared. 'Well, surely you've brought a gown for the catwalk parade, and an outfit for your song-and-dance routine?'

'No. No, I haven't.'

'I don't see why you're even here,' said Miss Cute Candy. 'What's the point of showing up if all you're going to be is One Big Nothing?'

It was another really rude remark, though Bonny could tell that, just like Miss Stardust, she wasn't trying to be nasty; she was just curious. But, even so, the idea of being One Big Nothing wasn't nice. It was quite obvious that showing up at Charm School without a pile of the right stuff was just about as hopeless as turning up at Practical Parenting without a baby. But what was so special about dressing up? These girls were all swanning about as if just looking your prettiest gave you the right to act as if other people were just grease spots on the carpet. You'd have a whole lot more right to strut around, Bonny thought sourly, if you could actually do something clever.

Do something clever ... Her brain was ticking over fast now. She'd have a horrible day if she let anybody know that she was here for Charm School, that was for sure. They'd already spotted her for a total loser. Even the man who stepped in the lift had thought she must be wandering around on the wrong floor, unless she had come to help someone called Maura with—

Bonny stared down at Miss Cute Candy's beautiful twinkling dancing shoes, and her own plain old sneakers. And in one brilliant diamanté flash came inspiration.

'I'm not here for the same reasons you are. I'm only here to give a hand with the sound and the lighting.'

'Oh, you're just one of Maura's little helpers!' Miss Cute Candy didn't just manage to make this sound as if she found it a much more likely idea than Bonny on a catwalk. In her keenness to let Bonny know exactly what she wanted in the lighting line, she spoke as if Bonny were some little garden gnome brought to life, just for the day, to be useful. 'Now look here, quick!' Grabbing Bonny's arm, she spun her round to face the mirror that ran the whole length of the wall. 'See all those horrible lumps? Well, what I want you to do is fix up the lighting so—'

'What horrible lumps?' asked Bonny, mystified.

'Those!' Miss Cute Candy said, pointing.

So Bonny looked again. All she could see in the mirror was herself, the flat grey wall behind, and Miss Cute Candy in her silky yellow dress and diamanté slippers, like an exotic spring flower rising, willowy and graceful, from a spangled pool.

'I can't see any lumps.'

Miss Cute Candy patted at the folds of her skirt.

'These,' she said. 'The lumps on these great ugly tree stumps.'

'Are you talking about your legs?'

'Legs!' scoffed Miss Cute Candy. 'They're so huge, they're more like pillars in a multi-storey car park!'

Was she serious? One minute, she'd been lording it over Bonny as if she were Miss World and Bonny were some little goblin. And the next minute, she was panicking about the size of her legs.

And really panicking. This was no joke. There was a tremble in her voice, Bonny could tell. And she was close to tears.

Bonny suddenly felt sorry for her, just the same way she'd felt sorry for Angelica for worrying about winning.

'Don't be so silly,' she tried to comfort her. 'You look—'

But Miss Cute Candy was too upset even to listen. 'I look horrible. Horrible! I'm fat and hideous. My nails are a sight. My hands would look more delicate stuffed inside oven gloves. I've got the worst legs in the world. My stomach sticks out like a pig's belly. My hair's turned to straw. I'm ugly, ugly, ugly.' She made a face at herself in the mirror. 'Ugly!' she jeered again. 'I'm a horrible little gnome and my clothes look like jumble.'

♥28♥

'Jumble?' This was beyond ridiculous. 'How can you say that your clothes look like jumble? That dress looks to me as if it comes from one of the smartest shops in town. And those sparkly slippers must have cost a *fortune!*'

But Miss Cute Candy was still staring despairingly into the huge wide mirror.

'It's not the clothes. They're all right, I suppose. It's what they look like on me. They do look like jumble. I bulge out all over, I'm so fat.' She started beating at her thighs with bunched-up fists. 'Fat, fat, fat! That's what I am. Fat!'

Bonny was mystified. Was this one of the little tantrums the tea boy had mentioned when he called Miss Cute Candy a tiger? But she didn't seem at all tigerish to Bonny. She seemed *desperate*. So maybe Bonny should rush down to Bookkeeping (Advanced) and fetch her mother, who could come up and say what she always said to Bonny when she was being silly about her hair, or her face, or the shape of her body.

Or Bonny could just try saying it herself.

'Don't be so soft. You know you're beautiful.'

'I am not! I am *not!*'

But how could Bonny go on and say the next bit? How could you say to someone whom you hardly knew, 'Well, you are to *me*! And even if you weren't, I wouldn't care. Even if you were the worst-looking person in the world, with a face like a squashed tomato and a body like a car wreck, I'd still love you so much I could burst, and so will everyone who ever gets to know you.'?

You can't make a speech like that to someone you've only just met, even if you know it backwards. And Bonny did. She'd heard her mother saying it a thousand times. She'd heard it when she came home from nursery school crying because Robert said she had a face like his toy bath duck. She'd heard it after she won the painting prize, and Estelle was jealous and whispered to everyone that Bonny looked like a maggot. She heard it from her mother over and over the year she was in Mrs Hamilton's class, because Mrs Hamilton never bothered to stop people being mean to one another, and Flora and her gang picked on all the other girls, giggling in corners, and saying horrible things about their hair and their clothes and their faces. And,

♥30♥

now she thought about it, she'd heard it only a few weeks ago, when she came home from her music lesson.

'What's up with you?' her mum had said. 'You look like a wet afternoon in Wolverhampton. What's the matter?'

'I'm all right.'

'Bad lesson?'

Bonny shook her head. 'It was all right.'

'Perhaps you're not feeling well.'

'I'm all right.'

She'd tried to get away to her bedroom, but Mum had caught her as she rushed past, and turned her round to look at her.

'Well, *something*'s not all right,' she'd said. 'Or you wouldn't be looking as if you're about to spill teardrops on my freshly mopped floor.'

And Bonny had burst into noisy sobs, and told her all about Mr Spicer poking his head out of the teaching room, and saying, 'You're a big beefy girl. Be an angel, and carry this cello along to the hall for me.'

'Yes ...?'

Mum was still waiting, Bonny could tell.

'That's it!' she wailed. 'He called me a big beefy girl!'

'He meant strong enough to carry a cello.'

'*Beefy*, he said!'

And Mum had had to swivel her round and point her at the mirror. 'Look,' she said. 'See that stranger? Is she so big that people step off the pavement when she comes along?'

'No,' Bonny said sullenly.

'Do people point at her? Or even stare?'

'No,' Bonny admitted unwillingly.

'Listen,' said Mum. And then she'd made the exact same speech she'd been making since Bonny was four, finishing up, as usual: 'You may not be perfect, but you're perfectly normal. And only dolls are perfect.'

Well, Bonny could at least say that to Miss Cute Candy. 'Only dolls are perfect.'

Miss Cute Candy rolled her eyes. 'Oh, really? Well, what about all those photos of the Curls and Purls Girls on the wall outside?'

The Curls and Purls Girls! The very sound of it made Bonny want to stick her fingers down her throat. 'Oh, *please!*' she said. 'Little Miss Airhead! Sweet Miss Empty-Brain! It's out of the Ark, this idea of dressing up for the afternoon as Miss Baby Perfect, with a frozen dolly smile and concrete sprayed hair. Who cares which one of the Little Miss Dippy Circle—'

'Little Miss *Pretty* Circle,' Miss Cute Candy corrected her sharply. 'Get it *right*.'

'Why? Are you in it?'

'I'm not just *in* it,' Miss Cute Candy said. 'I'm Cindy-Lou Brown, the secretary! And you needn't be rude about it. It's been going longer than any club you're in, I'll bet. My older sisters were both in it. And so was my mother. And so were both my aunties. One of them was even Miss Sparkling Sue.'

'But that's what I'm *saying*,' said Bonny. 'Who wants to worry about who wins some silly competition that was started way back when dinosaurs were roaming the earth, and Mrs Opalene was young? It doesn't have anything to do with real people living real lives. I bet there's no-one, even in this room, who could look perfect all day every day. Because, like I told you, only *dolls* are perfect.'

'Well, that's just where you're *wrong*!' snapped Cindy-Lou. Irritation fought with envy, and won. 'Because *Amethyst's* perfect. *And* she's not just good at winning practically every Little Miss Pretty Circle competition. She's also one of Mrs Opalene's pets in Charm School as well.'

'Which one is Amethyst?' Bonny asked curiously.

Cindy-Lou pointed to where a girl with a shimmering waterfall of hair was putting chairs in a circle round a sign that said, in bright gold lettering:

MRS OPALENE'S HANDY HELPING HINTS

'That's her. She's getting ready for the Beauty and Grooming tips.'

'Why would she bother with those,' Bonny tried to catch Cindy-Lou out, 'if she's already perfect?'

'You've got to keep up,' Cindy-Lou told Bonny sternly. 'Fashions and styles keep changing so people who aren't paying attention get left behind. That's why some of the girls from our Little Miss Pretty Circle come here to Mrs Opalene's Charm School every Saturday, and not just for her big Curls and Purls Competition. Mrs Opalene's really good at giving people all those special little tips that make the world of difference.'

The world of difference! Bonny stared. But just at that moment, as if to show how very keen she was not to miss any of these quite amazing tips, Cindy-Lou abandoned Bonny and rushed off to take her place in Amethyst's perfect circle of chairs even before Mrs Opalene had clapped her hands for attention.

'Girlies! Girlies, it's Beauty Tip time! Now I'm starting today with a small variation on that old idea of bleaching your elbows by sticking them in two halves of squeezed lemon.'

Bleaching your *elbows*? Bonny crept closer, fascinated.

Mrs Opalene waved a stern finger round the circle of girls who had hurried to their seats and pulled out their notebooks and pens. 'And I hope I don't have to remind anyone here that, *contrary* to what we read in some cheap and nasty little magazines, we don't use up our leftover lemon juice in the last clear rinse of our hair wash. And why not, Amethyst?'

Amethyst flicked her hair shyly. 'Because it strips it of the natural oils?'

'That's right, dear.'

Amethyst flicked her hair again, pleased.

'*Well*,' said Mrs Opalene, twinkling with enthusiasm. 'Some *very* clever person has worked out that, while you're sitting with your elbows in your lemon halves, you could be doing something inordinately useful at the same time.'

She gazed around at them. 'Can anybody guess what that might be?'

It seemed an easy enough question. 'Reading a good book?' suggested Bonny.

Mrs Opalene waved a beringed hand. 'Do try not to be silly, dear. This is seriou—' She broke off, inspecting Bonny properly for the first time. 'You look a little ...' She paused, puzzled, as she eyed this newcomer to her class up and down from plain old top to plain old toe. 'Dear, you don't seem quite ...' Again, she stopped, and peered even more closely. 'Are you *supposed* to be here?'

'Yes,' Bonny said, fingering the ticket in her pocket. She was about to explain when Cindy-Lou called out from her side of the circle.

'She's here to help Maura with the sound and the lighting.'

At once, she was the most popular person in the universe and everyone was calling out.

'Oh, please! May I just tell you something?'

'I have to explain to you exactly what I need.'

'Listen, there's a bit in my music where—'

'When Maura gets to the lighting for my bit—'

'You see, I have this problem with—'

'Girls! Girls!' Mrs Opalene clapped to hush them. 'Everyone will get their turn to visit the back room.' She turned back to Bonny. 'Well, dear,' she said. 'You do look awfully young to be dealing with expensive equipment. But I suppose if Maura thinks it's all right—' She gazed around. 'Has anyone seen Maura this morning?'

Most of the faces looked blank, though one framed by a mass of midnight blue ribbons began to crease, as if some worrying, half-remembered message was drifting to mind.

'Don't screw your face up, dear,' Mrs Opalene reproved her. 'It will only encourage early wrinkling.' And then, as if this reminded her of all she had to get through that morning, she impatiently waved Bonny out of the circle. 'All right, dear. Off you go.'

And Bonny, equally reminded of all she wanted to miss, sprang to her feet, delighted at this chance to flee from all their drippy lectures about bleached elbows and natural hair oils. The tea boy was right. They were ridiculous, perched in a circle on their little chairs, like fairies waiting for some wonderland party.

But Miss Stardust had jumped to her feet as well.

'Oh, please let me go with her,' she begged Mrs Opalene. 'Just so I can explain about my flashing lights.'

'Not yet, dear, because I'm sure Miss—'

She stopped and peered at Bonny, waiting for a name.

'"Sparky",' bossy Cristalle insisted, nodding her puffy hair. 'You always call electricians "Sparky". It's a theatre rule.'

'*Miss* Sparky,' reproved Mrs Opalene. 'I'm sure we don't *ever* want to forget our manners.' She turned back to Bonny, still peering, and started rooting in her bag. Bonny was sure that she was searching for her spectacles, and when she put them on she'd see at once that, even for somebody's helper, Bonny was terribly young – no older than everyone round her.

But then Miss Stardust started up again. 'About my flashing lights—'

'No!' said Mrs Opalene. 'Right now we're busy with our Handy Helping Hints. And since no-one's seen Maura yet, Miss Sparky had better start getting everything set up and ready for our rehearsals for the Curls and Purls Show.'

Bonny was horrified. What she'd been hoping to do was sneak away to find her mother. Vanish and never come back. Mum might have given her that stern look over her spectacles, and ordered her back with a lecture on not wasting money – warmly applauded, probably, Bonny thought bitterly, by all the other people in Bookkeeping (Advanced). But even then she could have spent the day lurking in some cupboard, out of sight.

But now they were expecting her to walk the other way – to the door at the back of the room. And then start up lights and music by herself! She was no expert in anything like that. She knew how to use her own music equipment, of course. And she was as good as anyone else at flicking on a light switch. But running the sound and lighting for the rehearsals for a Curls and Purls Show – even making things flash for Miss Stardust – well, that was different.

Better confess that she was really here, like all the rest, to listen to the Handy Hints.

But just at that moment Mrs Opalene spoke up again.

'So, dears. Back to all this time we have to spare, sitting with our elbows in our lemons. What are we going to do with it? Well, one quite *brilliant* idea is to make sure our feet are busy soaking in a bucket of perfumed water to soften all that nasty hard skin that gathers at the back of our poor heels!'

Bonny looked round. No-one was sniggering. No-one was rolling their eyes. No-one was even making a face of mock astonishment. They were all diligently taking notes.

Bonny turned round and set off determinedly for the back room.

Better Miss Sparky than Miss Twink.

CHAPTER TWO

The small back room looked like the cockpit of an airplane. There were switches everywhere. Switches to the right of her, switches to the left, and switches on the panel under the glass window through which she could see Mrs Opalene lecturing everyone on how to cope with all that nasty hard skin at the back of their heels.

And watching her.

Should she just sit there pretending? When Maura turned up, she could just say that she'd been looking for a phone or some water, and slip away.

Or should she have a go? After all, Maura might be very late. Or she might even have forgotten she was supposed to be there at all.

Bonny looked up. There on the panel right above her head was one big red master switch, labelled POWER.

No point in being chicken, Bonny thought. She flicked it down. At once, a hundred lights began to blink at her, red, white and green.

'Oh, excellent!' she breathed. 'Oh, yes! That's power!'

STORM o
Tempest o
SNOW ⇨
Thunder o
Sleet o
Fog o
Bit of drizzle o
Downpour o
Cats & dogs o
Very Windy o
Lightning ⇨

Taking the swivel seat, she whirled around. Best to get going. She might as well start with the panel in front of her. Just like any kitchen or toolshed, the things that were closest were probably the most useful.

Choosing a switch, she slid it gently up its track. Instantly, from the loudspeaker on the wall behind, she heard Mrs Opalene's voice, clear as a bell.

'So I certainly hope I don't have to remind anyone here—'

Bonny slid up the next switch. Mrs Opalene's voice turned deep and resonant. Almost booming.

'—that they should never, *ever* miss the chance of putting slices of fresh cucumber—'

Bonny slid the switch down again and pushed up the one on the other side. The voice went high and tinny.

'—on their eyelids. It isn't just refreshing—'

So that was the bass and the treble sorted out. Bonny switched Mrs Opalene's voice back to normal.

'—it also makes the *world* of difference.'

For heaven's sake! thought Bonny. There it was again, that silly claim, 'It makes the world of difference'. What was the matter with them all? Did they have maggots for brains? When did you ever bump into someone on the street, and think, Oh, look at those eyes! She must have been lying under cucumber slices? Distracted as she was by all the switches she was pushing up and down, still Bonny couldn't help muttering sarcastically, 'Oh, yes! Spit in my eye and then tell me it's raining!'

They heard it in there, she could tell. Everyone's face swivelled to stare at her through the huge glass window.

'Sorry!' called Bonny, switching off the blinking light labelled SOUND OUT.

She left SOUND IN still blinking.

So, for all the embarrassment, at least that was one more of Maura's little tricks under her belt. She turned to the buttons beside her. The first ones she pressed lit up the stage in dazzling circles.

'Spotlights!'

She tried more. This time, the whole front apron of the stage was bathed in a silver glow.

'Floodlights,' muttered Bonny.

She pressed a few more buttons and watched as huge, spotty red and green explosions bounced off the drapes on each side of the stage. On the backcloth behind, a waterfall appeared from nowhere, rippling down to a pool of foaming water.

'Special effects!'

She looked down. Inside the boxes at her feet were discs of every colour. And stencils, too. Some were cut into shapes she recognized, like windows or trees, and others were just cut into the strangest patterns. She picked out two and stared at them, trying to imagine what they would look like cast up on the back of the stage, lit up and enormous.

'Oh, yes! This one's a snowstorm! And this one is clouds.'

She was just peering through the next one – creepy forest branches? – when she was startled by a whisper from a loudspeaker overhead.

'Oh, no! Oh, no!' The voice was aghast. 'I ate it! I just ate it!'

Bonny spun round to look through the glass. Beside one of the microphones she must have left switched on, there were two latecomers she hadn't noticed. They'd stopped to stare at one another in the middle of changing their shoes.

'Oh, Cooki! You didn't!'

'I did, Lulu! One minute it was in my hand, and the next it was gone. I must have eaten it. I *must.*'

Poor thing! thought Bonny, remembering all too clearly how she'd felt when Herbie Stott slid a dead ant into the icing on her fairy cake and didn't tell her till she'd finished it. And when she'd gone to take the second bite of that apple Granny gave her, and saw the maggot hole – one swallow too late.

Lulu was looking horrified. 'You never ate the whole thing. Not *the whole thing.*'

'I must have, without noticing.'

'Cooki, how *could* you? They're *enormous*. How could you not even notice you were gobbling a whole biscuit?'

'I don't know! I don't know!' Cooki was almost in tears.

Bonny peered through the glass at this strange pair. A biscuit? How could you possibly get so upset about eating a biscuit? And if you went round acting as if scoffing one miserable biscuit was just about as terrible as eating your own granny, then how could you stand to have a name like Cooki? It would drive you mad.

She could flick on the SOUND OUT switch, and ask. But Mrs Opalene was on to yet another handy hint.

'So we never waste time at a bus stop! Wherever we are, it's exercise, exercise! We could be pulling in our tummy muscles. We could be swirling our ankles round to keep them trim. We could even be doing little knee bends to work on those flabby thighs—'

Bonny was baffled. None of the girls in the circle had thighs that looked any thicker than toast, and even Mrs Opalene was wearing such a gorgeous floaty skirt that no-one with a brain worth waking in the morning would waste time wondering about the legs it hid. Cupping her chin in her hands, Bonny gazed out through the glass. 'Batty!' she muttered to herself, shaking her head. 'Totally batty, the whole lot of them.'

She heard a voice behind her. 'Well, that's what happens to people who won't eat properly. First they waste away. Then they go mad.'

Bonny spun round. It was the tea boy again. He'd slid in silently and was putting two biscuits on a plate down on a ledge.

'Maura's mid-morning snack,' he said, pointing. 'Shall I leave you a couple as well, or are you—?'

'Oh, goody!' Bonny was already stretching out for the packet he was offering.

'Well, look at you!' the tea boy said admiringly. 'Straight in the trough! I can see you won't last all that long up here on Planet Snack-on-Air.'

Bonny couldn't help grinning. It wasn't the most polite thing to say – straight in the trough! – but it did prove to her that there was at least one other person in the world who thought this place was Crazy Club.

'Who are you?'

'I'm Toby. Being the tea boy is my Saturday job.' He sighed. 'Though I hate it so much I could practically *die*.'

'Why do you do it, then?' Bonny asked curiously.

'For the money, of course. I'm saving for a new violin.' He sighed again, even more heavily. 'Though sometimes I'm not sure it's worth it, trailing up and down these corridors all day just to make the music I play sound a little bit better.'

'It can't be too bad,' Bonny pointed out. 'Just dishing out the tea and biscuits.'

'And wisdom,' Toby pointed out. 'Don't forget wisdom. I can dish that out, too.'

Bonny laughed, pointing through the glass. 'If you're so wise,' she said, 'then tell me this. What's wrong with all of them? Why are they all the way they are?'

'I blame Mrs Opalene,' said Toby. 'Her words fly in one ear, and all their brains fly out the other.'

They both broke off to listen.

'As good as poison!' Mrs Opalene was warning everyone. 'Just fat and chemicals in fancy wrappers!'

'What is she on about now?'

'Possibly the cheaper range of my biscuits,' Toby admitted. 'Or sweets and crisps. She's got a bit of a thing about them.'

'That's not so odd. My mum and dad go on about them all the time.'

'Oh, everyone gets that,' said Toby. 'But Mrs Opalene acts as if one sweetie will blacken and rot your insides, and one little chocolate bar will make you swell till you explode.'

'And Lulu and Cooki act as if they believe her.'

'They all do.'

'I don't know why,' said Bonny. 'After all, Mrs Opalene's not exactly a beanpole herself. And she looks healthy enough.'

'Yes,' Toby agreed. 'Plump and cosy-looking.

And it suits her. So why she's so determined to starve these poor followers of hers into staircase spindles, I really don't know. But she never lets up. She's like some mad general, always going on about the Great Food War. You listen.'

He switched Mrs Opalene's voice up till it filled the room.

'So,' boomed the exultant tones. 'We're going to make two precious lists. On one, we're going to put all our Food Friends.' Mrs Opalene beamed. 'All those Handy Little Helpers to Happy Health. Like—?'

She waited.

'Raw vegetables!'

'Grilled fish!'

'Skimmed milk!'

They were all clapping in delight.

Mrs Opalene's face darkened now, and her voice went sombre. 'But on the other list, we're going to put all our Food Enemies. All those horrible, fatty, worthless—'

'Food Fiends!'

Some of them were even hissing.

'Chips!'

'Chocolate!'

'Fry-ups!'

'Sweet drinks!'

'Ice cream!'

And, in a wail of misery from Cooki, 'And horrible sneaky biscuits that creep up on you when you're not even looking, and practically *throw* themselves into your mouth.'

Bonny turned to the tea boy. 'I hope it's not catching.'

He picked up the empty biscuit plate. 'It looks as if you've been safe enough so far.'

'Did I eat Maura's as well? I am sorry,' Bonny said. 'I didn't notice.'

'That's because you're not yet under the spell. So just be careful. Block your ears till I come round again.'

He left to go back to his trolley just as Mrs Opalene changed tack.

'And now, dears,' Bonny heard her saying. 'We're going to spend a bit of time practising our sitting.'

Practising sitting! Bonny rolled her eyes. She hadn't practised sitting since the last time she fell off her potty, and she wasn't going to start again now. Switching Mrs Opalene's voice down to a soft burble, she turned to the nearest big floor lamp and tried to work out which of the knobs made the beam of light blur and sharpen, and which faded it out slowly or snapped it off fast. She'd just learned how to slide the colour sheets in front of the light beam when the door flew open. It was the girl whose hair was a mass of midnight blue ribbons. From her hand trailed a white shawl spangled with crystals like sunlight glittering on a heap of snow.

Coolly, she leaned against the doorway.

'Is that seat you're on comfy enough?' she asked, pointing at Bonny's swivel chair.

'Yes, thank you,' Bonny said, pleased someone cared. 'Very comfy.'

'It's not too grubby?'

'No.'

'There aren't grease spots all over it?' said the girl, concerned.

'No, really. It's fine.'

'What about the draught? Is it messing up your hair?'

'No, I don't think so.'

'Right,' said the girl. 'Hotch off, then. I'll sit there.'

Resisting the urge to shove this pushy visitor over backwards, Bonny said frostily, 'Are these the sort of manners you've learned in Charm School? Because, if they are, maybe your mother should ask for her money back.'

'And maybe yours should send you back where you came from.'

'Oh, yes?' challenged Bonny. 'And where's that?'

'Well, from the look of you,' the girl said, 'I'd say, The Land of No Style.'

'Better,' said Bonny icily, 'than crawling here from The Land of No Manners.'

The girl was pointing now. 'You realize the pattern on that blouse looks like a skin disease?'

'You obviously missed the class called Secrets of Flattery.'

'That mop on the top of your head doesn't even look like hair.'

'And no-one could possibly mistake you for a nice person.'

The girl let rip now. 'Oh, go fry your face!'

'Nosebleed!' snapped Bonny.

'Squirrelbrain!'

'Superbrat!'

'Oh, wonderful!' Suddenly, to Bonny's astonishment, the girl flung her arms wide, shut her eyes tight, and spun round merrily on her toes. 'Oh, brilliant! That feels a whole lot better!' Opening her eyes again, she stuck out her hand and gave Bonny a huge friendly smile. 'Hi,' she said. 'Sorry about all that. But, really, it's not easy to go round being charming all day. Sometimes you find you have to run away for a few minutes to let off steam.'

'What?' Bonny said, baffled. 'Didn't you mean any of it?'

'Well, no. Not really,' said the girl. 'I mean,

I quite like your blouse. And your hair looks perfectly normal.' She looked a little wistful. 'I suppose I wasn't making it up about wanting to sit in the chair, though. I wouldn't mind a little go on that. What's your swivelling record?'

'Four times round,' Bonny admitted, getting off it. 'Then it grinds to a halt.'

'Have you tried winding it right down to base before you start?'

'No,' Bonny said. 'I never thought.'

The girl tossed her glittering shawl onto the ledge, out of the way, and together they peered under the chair. 'No,' she said sadly after a moment. 'See? It's got a sort of lock on it, to stop the seat base flying off the chassis.'

'You seem to know an awful lot about swivel chairs.'

'I know a lot about *every* sort of chair. Here in Charm School we spend an awful lot of time just sitting waiting.'

'And then you go home to stick your elbows in lemon halves and sit and wait some more,' Bonny couldn't help pointing out.

'Only because it really works!' In her enthusiasm to twist her elbows round to show Bonny just how nicely they were bleached, the newcomer accidentally knocked a switch that set Mrs Opalene's voice reverberating over and over through the tiny room.

'Oh, brilliant!' said Bonny. 'You've found the echo for me!'

Both of them listened. Through all the copycat repeats bouncing from the walls as they faded, they could still make out what Mrs Opalene was saying.

'You are all beautiful! You owe it to the world to smile, smile, smile!'

Smile! Smile! the walls reminded them. *Smile! Smile! Smile! Smile!*

'I'd better get back.' On hearing Mrs Opalene's voice, Bonny's beribboned visitor had lifted her head and straightened her back, and begun to point out her toes as if she were on the brink of dancing. Was this what Toby meant about falling under the spell, Bonny suddenly wondered. And she was sorry, because, until that moment, she'd really been getting to like her cheerful new visitor. Quickly, before losing her to Mrs Opalene completely, she switched the voice burbling out of the loudspeaker down to softer than soft, and said, 'Oh, please don't go. Not till you've told me your name.'

'I'm Araminta,' the girl said in a voice so lilting it sounded as if she were about to burst into song. 'But all my friends call me Minty.'

'Minty?'

The girl's eyes widened. 'Is there something wrong?'

'No.' Bonny was embarrassed. 'I was just wondering why so many of you seem to be named after your enemies.'

'Enemies?' The girl shook her head. 'I don't believe I have any enem—'

'Those Food Fiends,' Bonny interrupted to explain. 'Minty. Cooki. Candy. You're all named after things you're not supposed to eat.'

'I'm hardly going to be called Carrot, am I?' Araminta chortled. 'Or Celery. Or Cucumber.'

For the first time since she'd arrived in this strange new town, Bonny felt as if she were having the sort of conversation she used to have with her old friends. 'You could be called Lettuce,' she suggested. 'That's a name. Or—'

But Mrs Opalene's voice had raised itself above its own soft burbling. 'Araminta! I hope you're not wasting Miss Sparky's time in there. How long can it take to explain what you want for one little song and dance routine? Don't forget there are other girls waiting.'

Araminta leaned over the microphone on Bonny's panel. Bonny switched to Sound Out just long enough for her to coo, 'Coming, Mrs Opalene.' And when Araminta turned back, to Bonny's disappointment it was obvious that she didn't have any more time for friendly chatter. Her tone was now firm and businesslike.

'Now, listen. I'm going to be a dancing snowflake so I'll need a haze of glistening white with maybe a hint of blue to make it look even colder. And I'll need snowflaky light spangles swirling around me, to match the crystals twinkling on my shawl. But don't forget to keep my face in a warm spotlight or I'll look so awful everyone will die of fright.' She pointed through the glass. 'I'll go and stand where I'll be, and you do a lighting test.'

A lighting test! Bonny was horrified. She'd hardly worked out where anything was and how it worked, and now she was practically being examined in it! She'd be caught out at once. Firstly she'd look like an idiot. And then she'd almost certainly be frogmarched down to her mother in deep disgrace. Or, worse, sent back to the big room to fail at something even more difficult – being charming.

As casually as possible, she said to Araminta, 'I don't suppose you happen to remember what sort of lights and things worked best for you last time ...?'

'I wasn't a snowflake last time,' Araminta said. 'I was a cowgirl.' Then, sensing that under Bonny's careless shrug there was real disappointment, she added kindly, 'But Suki did sing a little Winter Frost Song the time before that. And if I remember rightly, Maura fixed things so that—'

She broke off and clapped her hand over her mouth, staring at Bonny. 'Oh, no! Maura! I *knew* there was something I was supposed to tell Mrs Opalene!'

Bonny's heart sank. 'Oh, no!' she wailed in turn. 'I bet you were supposed to tell Mrs Opalene that Maura can't come today to do the lighting and the sound.' She was about to add, 'And I'll be on my own here, all day,' but it sounded so terrifying, she couldn't even bear to say it.

'Oh, dear!' But was this Araminta looking guilty at forgetting a message even a toddler could have remembered without much trouble? No. She was halfway to giggling. 'Oh, I'm such a noodlebrain! It was the very last thing she said to me when I was helping her last time.'

Poor, desperate Bonny felt a glimmer of hope. 'Helping her?'

'Oh, yes.' Araminta waved at the boxes stacked across the floor. 'I always enjoyed helping Maura. I'm tidy by nature, you see. So I quite enjoy putting things away.'

Bonny could almost have hugged this cheerful, sparkling girl who might yet save her bacon. 'So do you know where everything is kept?'

'Most of it.'

'Show me!' challenged Bonny. 'Let's just pretend there's someone standing in the right place for a lighting test and show me how you would set things up.'

'I have a better idea,' said Araminta. 'Let's ask Pearl. She'll be happy to be our stand-in. Pearl loves getting out of Mrs Opalene's Handy Hints. She says they're—' She stopped and giggled. 'No, I mustn't say it.'

'Mustn't say what?'

'What Pearl says about Handy Hints.'

'And what *does* Pearl say?'

Araminta spread her hands in merry wonder. 'She says she thinks some of them are a tiny bit boring.'

Bonny made a sour face. Her disappointment was intense. Anywhere else in the world, she would have longed to make friends with someone as sunny and exotic, someone so wonderfully irrepressible, as Araminta. And the two of them had been on the very edge of doing something really different and exciting – getting through the whole day without Mrs Opalene even guessing that Bonny wasn't the *real* Miss Sparky (or even a Miss Sparky at all). But now Araminta had reminded her that it was hopeless. Hopeless! What was the point of even dreaming of doing exciting things or making new friends in this stupid, stupid Charm School?

'Yes, Pearl's quite wrong,' she said. 'They're not a tiny bit boring at all. They're *enormously* boring, and quite *ridiculous*.'

'No, they're not!' Araminta sounded quite hurt and stung. 'Why, Serena's sister followed Mrs Opalene's handy hint about never sitting in front of the television without first dipping your hands in vegetable oil and wrapping them in clingfilm. And she got a job holding plates up to the sunlight in a washing-up advertisement.'

'Is that why you're here?' Bonny couldn't help teasing. 'So you can get to hold plates up to sunlight too?'

But Araminta missed the tone of sarcasm in her voice. She was too busy lifting her pretty little hands and shuddering. 'Don't be silly! I've got ugly great paws like giant soup plates!' It sounded so familiar. For just a moment, Bonny couldn't think why. And then she remembered Miss Cute Candy slapping at her perfectly normal legs, and calling them car park pillars.

Araminta tucked her hands away behind her back, out of sight, and said winsomely, 'But it would be nice to be *some* sort of model ...'

Bonny gazed out through the glass. 'I expect they all think that.'

'Not all of them.' Araminta pointed round the circle. 'Serena's here because she wants to be an actress, and she thinks looking nice and being charming will help her. And Lulu's here because her mother always wanted to be a catwalk star, but then she missed her big chance by getting married and having babies.

So she thought Lulu might like to have a go instead. And Sarajane's here because she's friends with Lulu and they go shopping after. And Cristalle's here because her dad is a top banker and he thinks that a charming, well-dressed secretary who does her hair nicely can get higher up in her job.'

'Maybe if she spent less time on her hair and more on her studies, she could get to be a top banker too. Then she could tell *him* what to wear,' Bonny said crossly.

But Araminta wasn't listening.

'And Esmeralda comes because her sister used to come. And Suki just comes to show off. And—'

'Show off? Show off what?'

'Anything. Everything. Whatever's new, Suki always somehow has it. And Mrs Opalene talks about it during the fashion tips. I expect she's doing that now, because that's Suki, pointing to her necklace thing, and I've never seen that before.'

Araminta turned up the sound on the speakers, so they could both listen.

'You see, dears,' Mrs Opalene was saying. 'As I keep telling everyone, it's so important to make sure you keep up to date. Take Suki's new pearl choker. Another girl might have been happy to dig any old double strand of pearls out of her jewellery case. But, Suki, dear, tell the others what you read in last week's issue of *Model Miss*.'

Araminta and Bonny watched Suki toss back her glistening mane of hair, and blush becomingly.

'It said that pearl chokers with only two strands are,' she shook her head in horror, '"*Totally Yesterday*".'

There was a little buzz around the circle.

'Really? I didn't know.'

'I heard that, too.'

'Oh, how upsetting! I've only just saved up and bought one!'

'It's horrid, isn't it?' Cooki was sympathising with the shocked Serena. 'But Suki's right. I read it too, in this month's *House of Style*. It said that two-strand chokers are "from Tiredsville" now, and the only thing to wear is three-strand chokers.'

Mrs Opalene clapped her hands to try to put a stop to the gossiping. 'So, go on, Suki. Tell everyone exactly what you did to find a three-strand choker for your dance on Saturday.'

Suki shrugged modestly. 'I went to forty different shops.'

'*Forty?*'

'Oh, Suki! That's amazing!'

The girls had taken to chattering again.

'Twenty-two is the most I've ever been to, looking for something special.'

'Sarajane and I went round thirty once, looking for the exact right plum suede boots. But we were together, and it took us a whole *week.*'

'But Suki did it all in one day. She must have been shattered afterwards.'

'Talk about Shop Till You Drop!'

Suki tilted her head and smiled modestly. 'Yes, I was tired. In fact, I was so tired, I fell asleep before the dancing even started.'

'Never mind. At least you *looked* right.'

'Oh, yes. I looked right. I checked before I left home, and I looked exactly like all the girls in this week's *Model Miss.*'

'There!' said Mrs Opalene. 'What an example for us all! Not ten shops. Not twenty. Not even thirty. Suki went to forty shops to get exactly what she wanted. And what do we call that, girls?'

Bonny could think of one answer. But a

quick sideways glance at Araminta's seraphically devoted face warned her to keep it to herself. Besides, everyone in the circle beyond the glass had started chanting.

'That's *dedication*, Mrs Opalene.'

'That's right, dears. *Dedication*. And how important that is. We cannot hope to reach the heights of fashion without dedication. They're not called "the heights" by accident. Oh, no. We are like mountain climbers, and, to reach our goal, we need a combination of vision, and planning, and hard, hard work.'

She spread her arms.

'What do our friends across the Channel say?'

Everyone chanted again.

'*Il faut souffrir pour être belle.*'

Bonny nudged Araminta. 'What's that?'

'French,' Araminta said. 'It means: "*You have to suffer to be beautiful.*" It's our Charm School motto.' She laid her hand on Bonny's arm. 'Well,' she said. 'You tell me, now you've heard all that, can you really understand how Pearl can find it even a tiny bit boring?'

'No,' Bonny admitted honestly. 'I wasn't bored. I thought Suki's shopping story was *fascinating*.'

(As fascinating as any other amazing tale, she added privately to herself. Like people putting their heads in lions' jaws, or walking on tightropes over deepest canyons.)

But Araminta just looked thrilled that Bonny agreed with her. 'Oh, I'm so glad! The moment I saw you, I thought, "Here's someone I can tell things, and she'll understand". And I was right!' Ecstatically, she swirled. The white shawl glittered, entrancing Bonny into silence as Araminta twirled towards the door.

'I'll go and borrow Pearl to be our stand-in while I show you what I know about the lights. I'll tell Mrs Opalene that, since there's no sign of Maura yet, we need a little bit of help, just for a while. She won't be pleased. But she's got a marshmallow heart, so we'll get round her somehow.'

Bonny watched, still enchanted, as Araminta tripped lightly up behind the one she called Pearl, and patted her arm gently. As Pearl twisted in her seat to listen, her dark curls caught the light. Then her eyes sparkled to match, and in an instant she was on her feet, begging Mrs Opalene, 'Oh, please! You do say how nice it is always to try to be helpful! Do let me go and be the stand-in for them. Oh, please! Oh, *please!*'

Mrs Opalene looked anxious. 'But, Pearl, dear, we're just getting to the hints on how to make a face pack out of oatmeal. Surely you wouldn't want to miss that.'

Pearl cast around desperately. 'Suki could tell me all about it afterwards, Mrs Opalene. I could even copy out her notes. Or Cindy-Lou's.'

'Oh, very well, then,' Mrs Opalene agreed reluctantly. 'Just for a few moments, since Maura's obviously held up in traffic or something and this new Miss Sparky's having a bit of trouble finding her way around our lovely new equipment.'

Already Pearl was scrambling up onto the stage. Mrs Opalene looked shocked. 'Pearl, dear. Do go round and walk up the steps nicely,' she added hastily, with a shudder. 'I do think that would be a little more *charming.*'

Blushing, Pearl scrambled back down, and tried to walk in hurried fairy footsteps. Suddenly Bonny noticed that no-one in the circle had eyes for anyone but Pearl. Some had little smiles on their faces, and some were merely looking a bit smug. But it was obvious what most of them were thinking. In Pearl's great rush to get away from Handy Hints, she hadn't been walking as if she were on the brink of dancing. And when she was pleading with Mrs Opalene, she hadn't been talking as if she were about to burst into song. So that was two black marks for Pearl. She was a whole lot less likely to be crowned the Supreme Queen, and walk off with the glistering tiara.

While Araminta was busy settling Pearl into the right position, Bonny looked round the circle of smiles and wondered if they could really be as gloating and creepy as she thought. For if these Charm School girls and Little Miss Pretties couldn't help showing how pleased they were when someone forgot to act like a simpering princess for just two minutes, then what on earth would they be like the day someone in their class at school showed up with braces on her teeth, or a spot on her nose?

It was a nasty thought.

In hurried Araminta. 'Quick!' she said. 'Before Mrs Opalene loses her patience and orders Pearl back in the circle. Watch this!'

She took the swivel chair and spun to face Pearl through the glass wall. 'Look at her standing there. Perfectly normal. Right?'

'Right,' Bonny agreed, moving closer.

'Look,' said Araminta. She flicked a switch, and pointed. Now Pearl was standing on the stage with only a black smudge for a face.

'That's backlight shining from behind,' Araminta explained. 'So all you see is that weird halo of light round her hair, and a glow through her ears.'

'Creepy!' admired Bonny. 'Like when you shine a torch through your fingers.'

Araminta switched from the backlight to a lamp tucked between the side drapes. 'And now she's sidelit. She has half a face.'

'Like an eclipse.'

'Interesting,' said Araminta. 'But not what we want.' She flicked another switch. 'And neither is this,' she said sternly.

Suddenly Pearl looked bony and ill.

'How did you do that?' said Bonny. 'She looks *terrible*. She looks as if she just crawled out of her grave.'

'That's lighting her from underneath. It is about the cruellest thing that you can do, and if you try it on me, I shall break off your arm, and beat you to death with the soggy end.'

'Charming!'

'Oh, dear!' Araminta clapped her hands over her mouth and looked shocked with herself.

Bonny just grinned. 'I still think it's brilliant,' she said. 'Absolutely *brilliant*.'

'But I'm not singing a monster song,' Araminta reproved her. 'I'm being a pretty snowflake, don't forget.' She looked a little wistful. 'Though it would be fun ...'

Very fast, one by one, she flicked more switches. And by turns, one by one, Pearl went all grey and ghostly, then burst out again with rosy health, then turned so shadowy and sinister that she sent shivers down Bonny's spine.

'That is *amazing*!' breathed Bonny when Pearl's skin changed to pale green before her eyes, and Araminta somehow turned the boards under her feet into shimmering silver wave patterns. 'Show me again!'

'You'd better not do anything like this to me,' warned Araminta. 'What I want is this.' She pressed down a whole row of switches. Suddenly Pearl looked as luminous as an angel, with her skin all milky and glowing.

'Now she even *looks* like a pearl!'

'Yes, but watch this.' Araminta slid two of the controls up in their runnels till Pearl's face was transfigured with a soft pink blush.

'How did you *do* that?' breathed Bonny, mesmerized.

Araminta showed her again.

'That's what *I* want,' she said. 'But, don't forget, around me I must have a swirling snowstorm.' She dived into one of the boxes on the floor and drew out a plastic disc. 'No, that's not the right one,' she said, holding it up to the light. 'That's rain spatters on a pond. Where are the snowflakes?'

She rooted again, tugging out what she wanted. 'Here it is!' Bonny watched as she dropped it neatly into the slot in one of the lanterns, and flicked a switch to start it revolving.

'Look!'

Bonny swung round to the stage again. Poor Pearl was standing in a raging blizzard.

'Whoops! Too fast!' said Araminta, twisting a knob to settle the blizzard into a gentle swirl of fat white flakes. 'There! That's nice.'

'It's *wonderful*!' said Bonny. 'It's astonishing! I think you're the cleverest person I ever saw. You've got magic at a touch and the world at your fingertips.'

Araminta's eyes shone. 'If you think I'm good, you should see Maura in action. Maura can conjure up thunderstorms and set off avalanches. She can make sheets of lava bubble out of the tops of volcanoes, and thin coils of smoke trail up from chimneypots. She can send tumbleweed bouncing across the prairie and tornadoes spinning through cornfields. She can turn a baking desert into a flood, and a flood back into a desert.'

'All at the flick of a switch!'

Araminta spun round on her toes. 'Full moon. New moon.'

'High tide. Low tide.'

'Golden dawn. Blue dusk.'

'Bright day. Black night.'

'And then there's the sound! She has *everything*. Roaring winds. Birdsong. Car crashes!'

Hands locked together, they were both

spinning now, faster and faster. When Bonny narrowed her eyes, all she could see was Araminta in a swirl of glittering white.

'Brass bands. Heavenly choirs.'
'Gunshots. Explosions.'
'Children outside in the playground.'
'Breaking glass.'
'A baby whimpering.'
'Crashing surf.'
'A piano in a far-off room.'
'Trains hurtling past.'

'Church bells. Whistling kettles.'

'Street riots. Sirens. Crackling fires.'

Dizzy, they slowed to a halt, still holding hands. 'You must be mad,' said Bonny. 'You must be absolutely crazy.'

'Crazy?' Araminta looked baffled, and very hurt.

'Yes.' Somehow, Bonny couldn't help saying it. 'Crazy.' All of her earlier disappointment had swept back, and worse. All the long journey in the car alone with her mother she'd hoped so much that, in this strange new town, she'd find a friend – someone as sunny and sparkling and wonderful as Araminta. And now she'd found her. But, to keep her by her side, she'd have to spend at least half of her life drivelling on about things like five-strand bracelets and silver-pink nail polish, and whether flower earrings had somehow suddenly become 'Totally Yesterday' between last Wednesday and this Friday.

And it was such an awful waste of time. Too high a price to pay. So she tried yet again to explain to Araminta. 'Listen. It doesn't make *sense*. Here you are, with the chance to do all these amazing things, and build whole worlds around you. You could sit in that swivel chair and flick switches to frighten people out of their wits, or lull them to sleep with soft music. You have the power to do *anything*.' She spread her hands and stared at Araminta. 'And what do you choose to do?'

And then, in her exasperation and frustration, she startled herself by answering her own question rudely. 'You just choose to sit on your bum and hope you look prettier than everyone around you!'

Tears sprang to Araminta's eyes and glittered like the shawl. 'That is so horrible! And so *unfair*.'

Bonny felt terrible. But still, instead of saying she was sorry, she muttered sullenly, 'What's so unfair about it? Isn't it true?'

'No! No, it's *not*!' Araminta glared through her tears and cast round for some way of hurting Bonny back. 'And you're only saying it because you're jealous.'

Now this was irritating. *'Jealous?'*

'Of course!' Araminta curled her lip. 'You're only being horrible because you know that never in a million years could someone like you win Mrs Opalene's beautiful glistering tiara!'

Bonny said scornfully, 'And what on earth

would someone like me want with some stupid, blistering tiara?'

The colour rushed to Araminta's cheeks. 'Oh, right! Nothing!' She took a deep breath, and rushed on. 'Because it certainly wouldn't look right on someone with your cheap, raggedy-looking haircut, and your dull face, and those jeans that do absolutely *nothing* for your figure!'

'Because I prefer to spend the hours of my life actually living, and not just waste them fussing about every silly square inch of my body?' Bonny said loftily.

'And it shows!'

'Who's being horrible now?' taunted Bonny.

Araminta went scarlet with frustration. 'You started it!' she practically screamed. 'You said that I was *crazy*.'

Bonny knew only too well that this was her last chance to back down. And maybe she would have tried to make up again with Araminta. But, looking away for a moment, she caught sight of Pearl, still patiently standing waiting in the middle of the stage, her face quite blank, and, for all Bonny knew, her mind quite blank as well.

Oh, they were all the same, these silly,

silly, *empty* girls.

'And so you are! Quite crazy!' she ended up shouting back in her impatience. 'Sitting for hours in that lolly-dolly circle, with daft Mrs Opalene, learning about cucumber slices and oatmeal face packs.'

She'd gone too far, insulting gentle, friendly Mrs Opalene. Instantly, Araminta sprang to her beloved teacher's defence.

'It's better than being—'

She broke off. And Bonny knew she ought to let it go. But something made her push Araminta into saying it, like some tired, miserable toddler who, not allowed to have the toy she wants, breaks the one that she's holding.

'What?' she asked dangerously. 'Better than being *what?*'

'Nothing,' snapped Araminta.

'Go on! Spit it out!' jeered Bonny.

And Araminta cracked. 'All right!' she shouted. 'You're snooty and mean about all of us, and horrid about dear Mrs Opalene. So I *will* say it! It's better than being a nasty little scruffpot with no looks at all!'

They stared at one another, shocked, their fresh new friendship in tatters.

'Oh, go away!' said Bonny, close to tears. 'Go back to your pretty little circle and learn something really important, like how to moisturize between your toes.'

Forgetting her shawl in her upset, Araminta rushed to the door and wrenched it open.

'You act so superior,' she hissed. 'But if it didn't mean we'd have to have you back in the class, I'd tell Mrs Opalene right now that you're nothing but a *fake*. You go round so sure you know how everybody else ought to live. But you ought to try looking in a mirror. It's obvious you don't bother to do it very often, but you *should*, because you'll see something really interesting.'

'Oh, yes?' said Bonny icily. 'And what's that?'

'I'll tell you!' shouted Araminta. 'Oh, yes. I'll tell you! I absolutely guarantee that, staring back at you out of that mirror, you'll see—'

She darted forward. Down went her pretty painted fingertips to push up the volume and flick on the echo switch before she finished up triumphantly,

'—the meanest girl I ever saw!'

Round flew the echoes, round and round,
bouncing off walls and curdling the air.

'The meanest girl I ever saw!'

'Ever saw!'

'Meanest!'

'Meanest!'

'Meanest!'

'Meanest!'

CHAPTER THREE

As soon as the door shut behind Araminta, tears sprang to Bonny's eyes.

'That's it!' she muttered. 'I'm not staying here!'

Tugging at the door in her turn, she rushed out in the corridor. Where was her mother? She'd find her if she had to burst into every single room in the building, waking the babies in Practical Parenting and sending pens skidding in Copperplate Handwriting.

Hurrying round the corner, she bumped into Toby and his trolley.

'I've got something for you,' he said, and

held out one of her favourite Scoobydoo biscuits.

The stars on the wrapper winked at her temptingly. But Bonny was in no mood to be cheered by treats.

'I don't want it,' she said. 'I can't pay for it, anyway.'

'It's already paid for,' he told her, thrusting it in her hand. And it was only then she noticed the rubber band round it, holding in the folded note.

FOR SALE
One whole day in ghastly,
difficult, slave-driving, no-breaks
Bookkeeping (Advanced).
Will swap for one day being charming.
(Roll on 5pm)
Love, Mum

Bonny unwrapped the Scoobydoo and took a massive bite.

'Thanks,' she said, when her mouth emptied. 'I really, really needed that.'

'I know,' said Toby. And Bonny noticed he was looking at the note in her hand, not the chocolate bar wrapper. She guessed he'd seen her tears. She didn't care, though. She felt so much better. Good enough to grin at him cheerfully as he gave her a ride on his trolley back to her little room.

★ ☀ ♥ ☆

If she were the meanest girl Araminta had ever seen, Bonny couldn't help thinking an hour or so later, it was against some pretty stiff competition. In between five-minute visits from each of Mrs Opalene's 'Superstars' explaining exactly what it was she wanted later in the Curls and Purls Show, Bonny switched up some of the microphones dangling from the ceiling in the big mirrored room, and found herself overhearing one catty conversation after another.

Take Miss Stardust and Miss Rosebud. They both seemed nice enough when they were in with Bonny. But, as Serena walked past in the big room, they wrinkled their noses.

Curious, Bonny turned up the microphone over their heads.

'Poo! What's that awful smell?'

'So *sickly*. With just a touch of flower stalks left rotting in a vase.'

'I wonder where it's coming from.' Miss Stardust suddenly pretended to notice Serena glaring. 'Oh, golly!' she said. 'Is it your perfume, Serena? I had no idea. I'm so sorry if Esmeralda and I upset you.'

'Yes, so sorry,' chortled Esmeralda. She turned to Miss Stardust. 'We think it's a nice smell really, don't we, Angelica?'

'Oh, yes!' said Angelica, in a voice that meant, as clear as paint, 'Oh, no, we don't. Really, we think it smells about as pleasant as fresh manure'. But Serena was already hurrying away to the corner of the room, where she stood looking angry and upset for a moment before turning to Pearl, who was standing beside her in a faded old slip, unzipping her big plastic dress bag.

Bonny switched over to the microphone above Pearl's head.

'Pearl!' she heard Serena say. 'That is the nicest dress you've ever worn to Charm School!'

Pearl looked up, baffled. 'But you haven't seen it yet. I'm only just getting it out now.'

Serena's voice dripped with false innocence. 'Isn't that it, what you're wearing?'

'This?' Pearl stared down at the faded, raggedy old slip in which she stood. 'This is some old thing I borrowed from my mum because it doesn't show round the neck when I'm wearing my new outfit.'

'Really?' Serena clapped her hands over her mouth, and acted horrified. 'Oh, I am sorry! I thought it must be your new frock!'

Pearl plucked at it, horrified. 'You didn't mean that, did you? You didn't really think this was the nicest dress I've ever worn?'

Her face was crumpling with unhappiness.

'Of course not!' said Serena in a voice that clearly meant: 'Oh yes, I did. But I had better not admit it'. It was, thought Bonny, exactly the same mean trick to make someone feel bad that Angelica and Esmeralda had just played on Serena herself. Would Pearl catch on, and tell Serena off for spitefulness? Or would she run in tears to dear, kind, marshmallow-hearted Mrs Opalene? Surely she'd care if all her precious, charming girls began to claw at one another like cats in a sack.

But Mrs Opalene was busy sewing up a fallen length of Cristalle's hem, while comforting weeping Amethyst about a fleck of white in one of her perfect fingernails. So all Pearl did was drift away from Serena, looking very unhappy. Bonny's eyes followed her across the room, till she came to a halt behind Cooki.

For a while Pearl stood watching Cooki brushing her hair in front of the long wide mirror. Then she said kindly, 'Never mind. No-one will notice.'

Anxiously, Cooki spun round. 'No-one will notice what?'

'Your hair.'

'What's wrong with it?'

Again came that same wide-eyed stare and pretend voice of innocence. 'Nothing. Nothing at all. Forget I said anything. It doesn't matter.'

Cooki turned back to the mirror. 'Yes, it does. I want to know what you meant. What can you see? What's gone wrong with my hair at the back there?'

'Nothing. I *told* you.'

'But you just said—'

'Honestly, Cooki,' Pearl interrupted her sweetly. 'It looks *wonderful*. Especially from the back.' But even through the glass panel, Bonny could see the little smile on Pearl's face that clearly meant, 'But I'm just saying that. It doesn't really'.

And Cooki saw it too.

'It doesn't, does it? It looks silly. Or wrong. Or *something*.' Cooki was panicking. 'What *is* it, Pearl? Tell me!'

'It's nothing. Honestly.' And off floated Pearl, leaving poor Cooki staring in the mirror in dismay. Bonny felt like rushing out of the control room to slap Pearl hard. But then it would only be fair to go and slap Serena, too, for upsetting Pearl. And, after that, she should go after Esmeralda and Angelica for starting the whole thing off. What was the matter with them all? The children in Bonny's first playgroup, when she was three, had all behaved better than this. And what was Mrs Opalene thinking of, caring more about fallen hems and fingernails than about them all roaming around being hateful to one another? Was this what she meant by having to suffer to be beautiful? But why would it help to have everyone round you feeling totally crummy?

Unless, of course, it was some horrible way of passing the unhappiness on, like a plate that was too hot to hold. It couldn't simply be to do with wanting to be the Supreme Queen and walk off the stage crowned with the glistering tiara. Bonny had been in plenty of competitions. There'd been the canoe race at club camp. And the climb-a-rope contest at the sports centre. And even that poetry speaking final in the school hall. Admittedly, nobody burst into noisy sobs of grief when George's canoe rolled over, tipping him into the water on the last bend. And she doubted if anyone was really very sorry when, in the rope climb, Gillian lost her nerve and her grip at the same time, and cascaded down the rope to the floor. And everyone burst out laughing when Martin forgot the last line of his poem, and just stared bleakly into space. But no-one had actually gone around beforehand, trying to make that sort of thing happen. No-one had taken the time to think up ways of making all the others lose their confidence, before things even got started.

Perhaps they'd all been too busy. After all, canoeing and climbing ropes and learning poetry use up your energy, and take up time. But things were very different here in Charm School. The problem with trying to win the glistering tiara was that you weren't kept busy actually *doing* things. You were just trying to *be*. Be neat. Be graceful. Be ladylike. Be more beautiful. To end up being the Supreme Queen.

So they had too much time to stand and fret. There was Serena, wrinkling her nose over and over, as if she were still trying to work out if her perfume really did smell like rotting flower stalks. Pearl was fingering her new frock, clearly still wondering if Serena would think it was as horrible as all her other ones. And Cooki, worried stiff, couldn't stop craning to try to see the back of her head in the mirror. Bonny was really relieved when Mrs Opalene stepped up to the microphone, and called them all back to their places in the circle. As Araminta tripped daintily across the room towards her seat, Bonny held up the shawl, to remind her she'd left it. She didn't want to admit it to herself, but she was really hoping that Araminta would rush back, just for a moment, to fetch it and make peace.

But Araminta just glanced coldly in her direction and then turned away. And then she crossed the circle to whisper something in Suki's ear, and, to Bonny's embarrassment, Suki, too, stared coldly at her through the glass.

The two of them exchanged places, so Araminta had her back to Bonny. Bonny felt terrible. She was quite glad when Mrs Opalene chided both of them.

'Now hurry up, dears, *please*. It's time for our precious *Words About Beauty.*'

Everyone looked delighted. 'Oh, goody!' trilled Amethyst. 'I *love* Words About Beauty!'

'Who'd like to start?' asked Mrs Opalene. 'Who's found some lovely and inspirational words they'd like to share?'

'I have,' said Esmeralda. She stood up, clasped her hands and cocked her head winsomely to the side, and started declaiming:

'My evening star! Laura, your beauty shines
As far as yon dark, whispering pines.'

'Enchanting!' cried Mrs Opalene, clasping

her own hands to her glittering bosom. 'Enchanting!'

'Can I be next?' begged Cristalle. 'I have two lines from a lovely poem we did at school.' Like Esmeralda, she clasped her hands before saying it aloud.

'My lady is a jewel; her pretty eyes
Sparkle, as on her velvet couch she lies.'

Mrs Opalene's rings flashed as she flattened her hand over her heart. 'Oh, that is nice! *My lady is a jewel.* I do like that. Isn't that nice, girls? Don't you all agree?'

Everyone nodded. Cooki's hand went up. 'I've just remembered one.' Making sure her knees were together and her feet tucked away neatly, she laid her hands in her lap and flicked her hair back, just like Amethyst.

'Oh, Flora! So well-named! You are a beau-
teous flower,
Shimmering in loveliness through every
shower.'

'*Shimmering in loveliness,*' repeated Mrs Opalene. 'Doesn't everyone think that's beautiful? I do. I think that's quite inspiring. Thank you, Cooki, dear. Now, who else has a little gem to offer?'

'I do,' said Cindy-Lou, jumping to her feet. 'I found it in a book of verses my granny gave me.'

'Lovely, dear.'

Cindy-Lou spread her hands, and quoted, *'She walks in beauty, like the night.'*

'Oh!' cried Mrs Opalene. She seemed to Bonny to be in the seventh heaven of delight. 'Oh, how we would all like to hear someone saying that of us! *She walks in beauty, like the night.* Wouldn't that be something lovely to aim for? Thank you so much, Cindy-Lou, for sharing that with us. Now, who would like to be next?'

She was still looking hopefully around the circle when Bonny's voice resounded through the loudspeaker.

'So where was she going?'

Hearing her own voice booming back at her, Bonny clapped her hands over her mouth. She hadn't meant to speak aloud, let alone with her own microphone channelled through to the big room. But now Mrs Opalene was peering, a little baffled, towards the glass window.

'Is that you, Miss Sparky? Did you have a question?'

Well, Bonny thought, my mother did buy a ticket. I do have a right to ask one. And to get an answer.

'I was just wonder-ing where she was going,' she told Mrs Opalene.

Mrs Opalene was baffled. 'Who, dear?'

'This woman walk-ing in beauty.'

'*Lady*, I think, dear,' Mrs Opalene reproved her. 'And what does it matter where she was going?'

'I was just interested,' Bonny defended her-self. 'Perhaps Cindy-Lou knows.'

Cindy-Lou didn't. 'The poet doesn't say. He just goes on a bit about how beautiful she was while she was walking there. He doesn't say where she was going, or why.'

'Shame,' Bonny muttered. 'I started out quite liking that one. But that makes it quite as boring as all of the others.'

Everyone stared. Shocked to the core, Mrs Opalene gathered the floaty matching wrap of her gown closer around her shoulders as if a chill wind had run through the room. 'Sorry, dear? Did I mishear? Could I possibly have heard you say the word "boring" about our lovely, inspirational Words About Beauty?'

'Well, yes,' admitted Bonny, wishing to heaven that she'd kept her mouth shut.

'Beauty that shines like a star?' reverberated Mrs Opalene, as though the switches on the sound panel had all pushed themselves right up to FULL. 'Eyes that sparkle like jewels? Flowers that shimmer in loveliness? You call those—' Her bosom trembled. '—*boring*!'

Bonny was trembling too, now. But still she tried to explain. 'I didn't mean to be rude. It's just that none of those things the poets are writing about actually *do* anything, do they?'

♥97♥

'What do you mean, none of them do anything?'

'Well, they don't,' Bonny said stoutly. 'None of them. Flowers and jewels and stars. They just sit there, looking pretty, and twinkling and glowing. That's all they do, and it must be terribly boring.'

'But they're *beautiful*!'

'Oh, yes,' said Bonny. 'I agree they're all nice to look at. What I'm saying is that it's probably a lot more fun to *look* at them than to *be* them.'

They were all staring at her, open-mouthed.

'After all,' Bonny finished up determinedly. 'Even the lady who could walk in beauty like the night couldn't have been going anywhere very interesting or the poet would have mentioned it.' She was about to switch off the microphone and get on with reading the *Handbook of Sound And Lighting* she'd found in a heap of cassette tapes, when Sarajane spoke up.

'Well, obviously this lady couldn't have been going anywhere very exciting, or she wouldn't have stayed looking nice.'

'That's right,' said Pearl. 'If she'd been climbing up a mountain, she would have got all sweaty.'

'And if she'd been at a funfair, her hair would have been blown about,' said Cristalle.

'And if she'd been on a beach, her make-up would have melted and smudged,' put in Suki.

They were all at it now.

'You can't do very much at all if you want to stay walking in beauty.'

'No, you certainly can't. You might get grubby.'

'Or ladder your tights.'

'Or break a fingernail.'

'Or get stains on your blouse.'

'Or scuff your heels.'

'Or—'

Just as, exasperated, Bonny reached forward to fade out this catalogue of woes, a hand came down to stop her. It was Toby, who had once again slid in silently and was standing behind her.

'Oh, don't turn them off,' he begged. 'I'm listening. This is more exciting than any adventure story. What else could possibly go wrong with their poor clothes?'

He pushed Bonny's fingers so the volume shot up again.

'Or the pleats in your skirt might fall out,'

Angelica was fretting.

'Or you might lose one of your earrings,' warned Amethyst.

'Or your hem might——'

But Bonny couldn't stand it. Jerking her hand under his, she cut Cooki off in mid-wail, and swung round to face him.

'Is it time for lunch yet?' she asked hopefully.

'Nearly. I just came by to pick up your tea cup.'

Their hands collided on the way to pick it up. The cup spun off the ledge, splashing dregs on his jeans.

Clutching his head, the tea boy reeled dramatically round the little back room. 'Oh, no!' he shrilled. 'A spot on my pretty trousers. Now I shall have to go all the way home to change, and I'll be late for the party!'

Seeing Bonny giggle, he stopped, satisfied, and rubbed the dregs of tea into his trousers, where they disappeared. 'Good colour, grey,' he said. 'Hides everything.' He nodded through the glass window. 'Not like all those girly lemons and pinks.'

'Men do wear yellow shirts,' argued Bonny. 'And pink ones.'

'But they don't have to *go* with anything.

When one gets dirty, you just pull the next out of the cupboard. You don't have to waste half your life standing in front of the mirror, worrying.' He plucked at the shirt he was wearing and squeaked at Bonny. 'Now tell me the truth! Does this shirt look exactly right? Does the green go with the grey of the trousers?'

'Everything goes with grey,' Bonny said. But he wasn't listening. He was still doing his imitation. 'No, don't spare my feelings! If they're not an absolute match, I swear I'll trail round twenty shops till I find a colour that's *perfect*.'

'Twenty shops is nothing,' scoffed Bonny. 'Suki in there went round forty to find the right choker.'

'Really?' The tea boy peered at Suki through the glass. 'I think I'd just pick the one I liked best in the first shop, then go off fishing.'

'So would my dad,' said Bonny. 'Mum says that's why men's clothes are always the first things you come to in big stores. Because, if you had to drag them any further, they wouldn't go.'

'Too busy,' said the tea boy. 'Better things to

do than trail round shopping every time the fashions change.' He picked up the microphone and pretended to make a news announcement. *'To no-one's astonishment, men's favourite trouser colours will remain the easy-to-match, stain-hiding dark range, and their hems will stay at ankle length for yet another season.'* He grinned at Bonny. 'And, believe me,' he added, 'no-one will even notice.'

'Unless you forget to put them on.'

'Oh, yes.' He snatched up Araminta's shawl. 'Or if they're all spangly, like this.' Swirling it round, he held it flat against his body. 'Toby, the Glittering Man!'

'Very flash,' agreed Bonny, thinking how odd he looked. When Araminta wore the shawl, she'd just looked special – all dressed up and fancy. But Toby immediately looked like a clown, or an actor in a pantomime, or the comedy star of some Christmas Variety Spectacular. Bonny was used to seeing women glitter. (Just look at Mrs Opalene.) But men don't go round glittering unless they're inviting you to share a laugh. No-one takes seriously someone who is twinkling. Bonny realised for the first time why lawyers and bankers went to work in sober suits, and police officers and traffic wardens wore dark uniforms. It would be hard to pay them nearly so much attention if they were dressed in frothy clothes, with flashing rhinestone earrings. Trousers that twinkle say only, 'Look! Look at me!' Plain skirts and jackets (like Mrs Sullivan's at school) say, 'Now listen carefully. This is important.' Or—

The spell was clearly working overtime, because the next thing Bonny heard Toby say was, 'Hey! You're not listening!'

'No, sorry,' Bonny said. 'I was too busy watching you twinkle.'

'What I was saying,' repeated Toby, draping Araminta's shawl over the chair, 'is that lunch will be ready in five minutes.'

'Goody. I'm starving. I'll be first in the queue.'

'Which queue?' he asked. 'The queue for the smallest heap of beans? Or the thinnest slice of bread? Or the tiniest dab of butter?'

'Don't they even eat at *mealtimes*?'

'Eat!' Toby said. '*Eat*? Oh, you'll see one or two of them pushing the odd shred of lettuce around their plates, and nibbling at stalks of celery. You might even spot one of them looking longingly at a sliver of grilled fish; or gingerly dipping her spoon into a tiny tub of non-fat, low-calorie yoghurt. But what you and I would call *eating?* No, you won't see any of that.'

'*They* will, though,' Bonny said drily. 'They'll see *me*.'

They didn't simply see. They sat and *stared*. (All except Araminta, who stood as far from Bonny as she could in the long canteen queue, then took a seat at the far end of the table.) None of the rest of them could take their eyes off Bonny's double slice of pizza and her tossed salad.

Bonny took her first mouthfuls, and looked round in hopes of seeing her mother. But, clearly, the victims of Bookkeeping (Advanced) were kept miserably hungry as well as horribly busy. And, anyway, Pearl was tapping her on her sleeve.

'You do realize,' she was saying kindly, 'that that dressing you've put on your salad is mostly oil?'

Bonny gave it some thought. 'I can taste vinegar in it,' she said after a moment. 'And a little bit of garlic.'

'Yes,' chimed in Cindy-Lou. 'But Pearl is right. It's mostly oil.'

Bonny was mystified. 'What's wrong with that? Olive oil tastes nice. And it's good for you.'

'It's a hundred and fifty calories a *tablespoonful*,' said Cristalle firmly, as if that settled the matter. Simply to keep the peace, Bonny shifted her fork across to her pizza.

Suki's mouth dropped open. 'Are you really going to eat that?' she couldn't help asking.

'Yes.' Bonny stared at her. 'That's why I took it.'

Now everyone was chiming in. '*All* of it? *Both slices*?'

'As well as the salad dressing?'

'*Now?*'

'Those croutons look to me as if they're *fried*,' added Cristalle, as if the word meant '*poisonous*'.

Bonny tried to ignore them all. Keeping her head well down, she watched the food on their own plates. Toby was right. All that they seemed to do was shuffle it round and round, making a giant great fuss of it, but never actually putting any of it in their mouths. Bonny watched, fascinated, as Esmeralda made a great show of reaching for a slice of bread, then unwrapping her butter pat. It took her twenty times as long as it would have taken Bonny to peel the shiny foil off the tiny yellow square and fold the foil up neatly. Then Esmeralda picked up her knife and started to mash the butter on her plate.

'What are you doing?'

'Just softening the butter.'

'Why?'

'It spreads better,' said Esmeralda.

And thinner, too. Bonny watched Esmeralda smear the tiniest fraction of butter onto her bread, and make a great display of spreading it around, though there was so little of it, it was practically invisible.

'Aren't you using the rest up?'

'Gosh, no.' Esmeralda looked horrified. 'This is *tons*.'

She still wasn't actually eating it, Bonny noticed. Now she was neatly cutting the slice into quarters. And, after that, each quarter into strips. And then she trimmed each crust off, one by one. Anyone glancing her way would be left with the impression that she was bent over her plate tucking in happily. But she still hadn't eaten anything.

Bonny leaned over the table and tapped her fork beside Esmeralda's plate. In a nannyish voice, she said to her, 'Stop playing with your food, dear!'

Esmeralda looked up, startled. 'What do you mean?'

'Just what I say,' said Bonny, still in her nanny voice. 'Stop messing, and eat it.'

'I *am* eating,' said Esmeralda.

'No, you're not,' Bonny said, going back to her normal voice to explain what she meant. 'What you're doing is shunting and mashing and smearing and slicing. But you're not actually *eating* anything. So, apart from the fact that you're doing it so daintily, you're just messing with your food like a giant great baby.'

Esmeralda went scarlet. 'I am not! I *am* eating. I have eaten *tons*.'

'*What?* Tell us *what*.'

'I ate most of the lettuce. And the fishcake. And the beans.'

'You didn't eat the fishcake,' Suki said. 'You hid it under the lettuce. With the beans.'

Bonny reached over and lifted Esmeralda's lettuce with her fork. Esmeralda blushed as the evidence was displayed around the table. But several of the others were blushing too. Bonny turned to her right and lifted Amethyst's largest lettuce leaf with the fork. Out peeped two fish fingers and some mushrooms. She turned to her left, and Serena snatched her plate away.

'It's none of your business!'

'You have to eat,' said Bonny. 'If you don't eat, your brain doesn't work properly, and you get all tearful and crabby.'

There was a whisper further up the table, and everyone giggled.

'What was that?' asked Bonny.

'Nothing,' said Sarajane. 'Angelica just made a little joke, that's all.'

'What did you say?' Bonny asked Angelica.

'Nothing,' said Angelica.

'No, go on,' insisted Bonny. 'Share the joke.'

'I've forgotten,' said Angelica.

'I haven't,' said Serena, getting her own back on Angelica for being so spiteful about the smell of her perfume. She leaned towards Bonny. 'When you said that people who don't eat get all tearful and crabby, Angelica said,

"Better than getting all fat like her".'

'All fat like who?'

Everyone was silent. Even Araminta was watching now. And Angelica looked very embarrassed.

Bonny looked down at herself. 'Do you mean *me*?'

Still no-one spoke. Bonny pushed back her chair and looked at herself. She was the exact same shape she'd been when she left home that morning. She wasn't built from matchsticks, it was true. Her legs weren't thin glass rods. You couldn't have spread your hands round her waist and touched your own fingers.

But she wasn't fat.

She was perfectly normal.

Pushing her chair back even further, Bonny looked round the table.

'You should stop worrying about how much you have on your bodies,' she told them. 'And start worrying about how little you have in your heads. No wonder the tea boy calls you all Twinks.'

'*Twinks*?'

'Toby?'

They were outraged.

♥110♥

'He does *not*.'

'Don't listen to her. She's just saying mean things to upset us.'

Bonny pointed a finger at Lulu, who was the last to speak. 'Oh, no, I'm not! Toby agrees with me. He thinks you're all silly and vain. And you *are*,' she added fiercely. 'You spend your whole lives trailing round shops, and parked on your bums trying to look prettier than the person beside you, and strolling round being spiteful to one another. So why should anyone think you have more than half a brain between you?'

Now Cristalle was shaking her finger back at Bonny. 'You're wrong!' she snapped. 'Quite wrong! Toby actually thinks that we're something rather special. That's why he spends as much time as he can watching us through the glass window.'

'Oh no, it's not,' said Bonny. 'He watches you because he can't get over how daffy you are.'

'How wrong can you get, Miss Clever Sparky? I tell you, Toby *likes* us.' Cristalle gave an arch look across the table to Sarajane. 'Especially *one* of us,' she added meaningfully. 'There does happen to be one of us he *really* likes ...'

At this, everyone turned to look at Sarajane, who blushed bright pink. But Bonny barely noticed. '*You're* the ones who've got it wrong,' she was too busy insisting. 'He doesn't *like* you all. You just *amuse* him.'

Sarajane's blush turned fiery red, and Esmeralda said loudly to no-one in particular, 'Talk about other people being spiteful! She should try listening to *herself*.'

There was another giggle and more whispering at the other end of the table. This time Bonny was quicker swinging round, and out of the corner of her eye, she saw Araminta dart a look at her, then hastily shut her mouth and wipe an amused smile off her face.

Bonny was astonished at how upset she felt – as if a real, true friend had turned against her. She felt tears gathering and her voice was shaky. 'I suppose *you're* being nasty about me now.'

Araminta looked horribly guilty. But it was Lulu at her side who broke the awkward silence. Putting on that sugared poison voice Bonny had heard so often that morning as people said their horrid things, she explained very kindly to Bonny: 'Oh, no. Minty was trying to be *nice*. You see, she was explaining to us all why you can't help being so rude and disagreeable.'

Minty! They all had one another as friends, and she had none! Miserable as she could be, Bonny said crossly, 'Oh, really? Why is that, then?'

As she spoke, she tried looking Araminta straight in the eye, but Araminta hastily stared down at the table. 'It doesn't matter,' she mumbled very uncomfortably. 'I've quite forgotten what I said.'

Once again, Miss Pass-on-the-Spite Serena pitched in to help someone who'd lost her memory. She leaned over to Bonny.

'*I* haven't, though. Minty was just explaining that you were simply jealous.'

'Jealous?' Now it was Bonny's turn to be outraged. '*Jealous?* Of all you noodle-brained *ninnies*? Of all you flopsy-mopsy *beanbrains*? Oh, I don't think so!' Then, suddenly remembering you couldn't trust what any of them said when they were causing trouble, she leaned across the table and said to Araminta, 'Is that *true*?'

Araminta flushed even redder than Sarajane had earlier. 'Is what true?'

'What she just said. That you told them I was jealous.'

Araminta didn't answer. Bonny rose to her feet. 'Is it?' she demanded again. 'Is it true? Is that what you said?'

Again, Araminta took refuge in mumbling. 'I've quite forgotten. I can't remember what I said at all.'

'You can't remember?' Bonny leaned over the table. 'Well, I did warn you, if you don't eat, your brain stops working properly.' She picked up her plate. 'What you need, Araminta, is a proper meal, and I've got one here for you!'

All Bonny's fury and upset boiled up in her. And boiled over. And before Araminta could even twist her head aside, Bonny had slapped the lukewarm plate of pizza in her face, and ground it round.

Everyone squealed, and Araminta clawed at the dripping mess of cheese and tomato and onion. Her huge shocked saucer eyes peered out in horror, like two rounds of pepperoni.

'There!' Bonny snapped. 'Feeling any better?'

And off she stomped, in a foul temper, out of the canteen and up the back stairs, all alone, back to Charm School.

CHAPTER FOUR

"You have to hand it to Mrs Opalene,' Toby remarked on his next visit. 'You start a riot, and before she's even finished ticking you off properly, she's somehow managed to turn it into a class about taking off make-up.'

And so she had. As soon as it became clear Bonny was stubbornly going to stick to her story of tripping as she so kindly cleared away Araminta's unfinished meal, Mrs Opalene had simply given her one last, helpless, reproachful look, then turned to poor dripping Araminta.

Holding her at arm's length, she said, with as much enthusiasm as she could muster:

'Marvellous! The perfect opportunity to try out some cleansers! Thank you, dear Araminta, for giving us a chance to do some real *testing*.'

Bonny felt terrible. She'd been so rude about poor Mrs Opalene. Yet here she was, valiantly making the best of things, scraping the worst of the pizza off with little balls of cotton wool till, gradually, Araminta's tearful face emerged through the tomato-stained cheese streaks.

'There! Splendid! Now we'll divide your face into four separate sections, and try a different cleanser on each, to see which comes out best.' She looked around. 'Now who would like to be first to show us their gentle cleansing technique?'

Araminta's sobs quietened as Pearl stepped forward eagerly. 'Oh, please! Can I have a go with that green glop?'

Mrs Opalene threw up her hands. 'That green glop! That green glop!' Lifting the tiny plastic tub of cream at which Pearl had been pointing, she rebuked her errant pupil. 'Pearl, dear, this is Glow Girl's phytolyastil

V.I.A. Complex tissue peptide VHJ with hygragscopic elements and natural ceramides, and a syntropic blend of unique Derma Bio Tropocollagen. You may not simply call it "glop".'

'Sorry,' said Pearl, chastened.

Toby nudged Bonny. 'Looks like glop to me.'

'And me.'

'Stroke it on *gently*, dear,' Mrs Opalene was telling Pearl. 'Don't *scrape* away at Araminta's precious face. And, as with all our little skin helpers, dears, what must we always remember?'

She waved her hands like a conductor as all of them chorused dutifully.

'*Smeary is dreary*, Mrs Opalene.'

'Smeary is dreary!' Bonny flipped off the sound. 'Phytolyastil!' she muttered scornfully. 'Tissue peptides! It's just pretend science, so they can charge the earth for every teaspoon. But Pearl's quite right. All it is really is glop.

And if everyone suddenly stopped feeling halfway to ugly, all those glop factories would close overnight.'

'Someone would lose an awful lot of money if that happened.'

'But everyone else would keep a lot more.'

'The factory owners ought to pay Mrs Opalene to run this Charm School,' Toby said. 'In come these perfectly normal girls, and only one of them can end up winning the glistering tiara. So all the rest go home feeling like rubbish, and buy more glop.'

'And clothes.'

'And jewellery.'

'And shoes.'

'And perfume.'

'And nail stuff.'

'And hair stuff.'

'And beauty books and magazines.' She stared at Toby, horrified. 'That's what it's all for, really, isn't it? To make them buy more stuff. On and on and on. And, if they're not buying fast enough, you simply tell them that swimsuits look different this year.'

'Or handbags have to be made out of raffia.'

'Or pink is *yesterday*'s colour.'

'It's like having an exam every day. And

every now and then you get to have a big exam, like this. One of them gets to come top and be the Supreme Queen.'

'And all the rest go home feeling ugly, and think they ought to try harder. So they waste even more of their time shopping, and even more of their money on stuff to try to look nicer.'

'And they can't even cheer themselves up by having two slices of pizza. They have to go round half-starved in case they put on a quarter of an ounce.'

'And think their legs have turned into pillars in a multi-storey car park.' She turned to Toby. 'It's very clever, really, isn't it? *Too* clever ...'

Toby eyed her curiously. 'What do you mean?'

'Just what I say. It's *too* clever. Hard to believe it's all a sort of accident.'

'You don't think someone *planned* it?'

'Wouldn't you?'

'Who? Some evil band of fat glop factory owners, sailing off on luxury holidays with all the loot they've made?'

'Laughing up their sleeves at all the silly people they've fooled into buying yet another set of clothes.'

'Because sleeves are much puffier this year.'

'Or skirts are much straighter.' She narrowed her eyes suspiciously. 'You know, I wouldn't be at all surprised if they owned all the glossy magazines as well. Wouldn't that be the cleverest thing? And wouldn't it be a cheek? First, you rip everyone off by selling them forty pages of "fashion news". And then you sit back and watch them trailing round the shops like sheep, ripping themselves off by buying stuff they'd never have thought of, without you.'

'No wonder they're laughing.'

Bonny turned to stare through the glass. 'Do you suppose that Mrs Opalene is in on it?'

'Mrs Opalene? In the pay of the glop men? Do you really think so?'

'I don't know.'

Together they watched Mrs Opalene. As usual, she was all excited about something. This time it appeared to be yet another of the pretty tubes and pots and bottles spread on the table top at her side.

Bonny flicked up the sound.

'... with lanoline filtrate and a specially selected cationic derivative ...'

Bonny flicked the sound down again.

'I don't know,' Toby said dubiously. 'She's never sounded like a fake to me. And she has such an honest face. I honestly think she *believes* it.'

'Sincerely? *All* of it?'

Now it was Toby's turn to flick up the sound.

'... with that super protein conditioning that does so much to adjust the P.H. balance and improve the *texture* of ...'

He flicked it down.

'She wouldn't have to be one of the gang,' he said. 'In fact, it probably works better for them if she truly believes everything she says.'

'Then she can't turn on them. Or spill the beans.'

'She'll just go round her whole life, spreading the word like a preacher.'

'*Smeary is dreary. You have to suffer to be beautiful*. Yes.' Bonny swivelled on the chair. 'It's about as clever a plan as you can get. You set it off with a few fancy photographs, and then sit back and watch people like Mrs Opalene rush in and keep it going.'

'Like unpaid police officers herding everyone along in the right direction.'

'*Walk as if you were dancing!*' Bonny mimicked bitterly. '*Smile nicely. Twirl neatly. Keep your knees together.* And when she's not around, there's all those little beauty helpers of hers to keep it going.' Again, she was mimicking. '*You're not going to eat* both *those slices of pizza, are you? Do you realize it's* fried? *You don't look as if you fell to earth from Planet Fashion.*'

'They can be a whole lot worse than that,' said Toby. 'At least the police have rest days. This lot never stop going on at one another, keeping themselves up to scratch.' He flicked on the microphones in the corners of the room, where Mrs Opalene's girls were scattering to get themselves ready for the Curls and Purls Show.

Both of them listened.

'I think you should get your hair highlighted again,' Serena was telling Cindy-Lou. 'It's beginning to look just that tiny bit mousy.'

'Perhaps the pink frock suits your colouring better,' Amethyst was suggesting to Angelica.

'Are those split ends in your hair?' Sarajane was asking Esmeralda. 'Maybe it's time for a trim.'

'Your hem's just the tiniest bit uneven,'
Lulu was warning Suki. 'Though it hardly
shows at all from the
front.'

Bonny shook her
head. 'I don't know
how they can stand
it. It's like listening
to dripping
taps.'

They
eavesdropped some more.

'Fat people should never,
ever tuck in their blouses,'
Cristalle was pontificating
firmly. 'It makes them look
awful. Just
awful.'

'You
should always
smile in a mirror
to check your teeth
after eating spinach,'
Pearl was telling
Araminta.

'You should never
wear aubergine eye

shadow with a pink top,' Cindy-Lou was explaining to Cooki. 'The colours simply *shriek* at one another.'

'Always rest your weight on your back leg, and point the other towards the camera,' Pearl was informing Sarajane.

'So many *rules*,' Toby said wonderingly. '"You must *always* ...", "You should *never* ...".'

'The magazines are full of rules,' Bonny told him. 'Well, not even rules, really. *Orders*. Don't wear this with that! Rub this in your face before you paint that on! Walk like this! Sit like that!'

'It was like that in my nursery school,' Toby remembered. 'Hang up your coat nicely! Put your wellies in the corner! Wash your hands before snack-time!'

'But you were *four*.'

'If any magazine I bought kept giving me orders,' Toby said, 'I'd chuck it in the nearest bin.'

'But they just try a bit harder.'

They watched Serena struggling into her outfit.

'They don't even buy clothes that fit them,' Toby observed ruefully. 'They force their bodies into fitting the clothes.' He pointed through the glass. 'Look at her face. She's astonished that she's managed to fasten that waistband.'

'No, she's not,' Bonny corrected him. 'She's just striking a pose. Esmeralda's probably just told her "amazed" is her best look and makes her eyes look big and round.'

Toby turned away in disgust, but Bonny couldn't help carrying on watching.

'They're like caged birds,' she said. 'The door's wide open, but instead of flying off, they spend their whole time making pretty Milly the Model poses on their perches, and fluffing up their feathers.'

'Mrs Opalene's been running this Charm School for years,' Toby told Bonny. 'Some of them must have broken out and got a life. Why haven't this lot followed?'

'Because they don't see why the others left. When someone decides, "This is a waste of time," and stomps off home to do something more interesting, all of them think, "Oh, she's just a bad loser. She's leaving because she knows she'll never win."'

'Perhaps they wouldn't be quite so happy to stay in their cages if you told them Mrs Opalene was part of a horrible plot to take their money and use up their lives.'

'They'd never believe me,' said Bonny. 'They all think she's wonderful – so kind and encouraging. Look how she didn't even order me out after the fuss with the pizza, in case there'd be no lights or music for their precious show.' Bonny pointed at radiant, shawl-swirling Araminta. 'Besides,' she added forlornly, *she's* already told them all that I'm just jealous.'

Again it came, that pang of something precious, lost for ever. She turned to Toby for comfort. But, he, too, was staring wistfully out through the glass.

'You'd think that, if you'd already managed to win that stupid glistering tiara of theirs at least once, you'd be able to stop bothering. But you take that lovely, raven-haired Sarajane. She was Miss Sweet Caroline *ages* ago. But still she seems to do nothing at all except worry about what she looks like.'

He looked so mournful that Bonny couldn't help remembering Cristalle's arch look at lunch, and Sarajane's blush. To try and cheer him she put her irritation with the girls aside and stuck up for Sarajane. 'She probably tries to think about other things. But then I expect she goes out and sees a hundred posters of pretty girls with slim long legs. Or she switches on the television and sees advertisements of girls with perfect hair. Or she goes to the cinema and sees dozens of actresses with beautiful faces.'

He made an impatient gesture. 'Someone should tell her the photographs are all touched up. And models go round practically *chained* to their hairdressers. And most of the adverts for tights and swimsuits have the models' legs stretched on computer, to look longer and slimmer.'

Bonny shrugged. 'I expect they've been told all that already. But just so long as somewhere in the world there's one perfect person—'

'One beautiful, hair-flicking Amethyst ...'

'—they'll all just keep on trying.' Bonny sighed. 'But you are right. Somebody ought to try and rescue them.'

'Not me,' Toby said hastily. 'I have to get back to the tea room before someone comes looking for me. And you should be getting on with sorting things out for their silly Curls and Purls show.'

'I suppose it's better than just sitting in here watching them. That's really sad.'

'Don't feel too sorry for them. That's what they like most, being looked at.' He pulled the door open. 'Feel sorry for their poor friends. Listening to people fussing about clothes and hair and how much weight they've put on is even more boring than being dragged around the shops watching someone look for clothes they don't need.'

Bonny grinned mischievously. 'Maybe some girls go to all this trouble to look nice for *you* ...'

He waggled a finger at her. 'Don't kid yourself. I couldn't give a bean. No, they're doing it to impress one another, and make a heap more money for the glop men.'

The glop men ... As Toby hurried off, Bonny turned back to the glass. Could it be some great conspiracy? Like Toby, Bonny found it hard to believe that Mrs Opalene's beaming, enthusiastic face masked some vile plan to steal people's money by making them feel awful. After all, boys and men wasted time and money too. Look at the hours and hours her father spent slumped on the sofa watching eleven men – or was it twelve? – kicking some stupid ball up and down the pitch, then listening to even bigger idiots drivelling on about how they must be "over the moon", or "totally gutted". At least the girls could sing and dance, and knew how to wear their clothes properly. The boy next door spent all his money on new football stuff, and his team changed it time and again. He didn't get to decide when to stop wearing it. The team manager decided for him. That was fashion too.

Her head was spinning. She was almost glad when bossy Cristalle poked her great puffy-haired head around the door and said to her officiously, 'Nearly time to start! Pass me that box, please.'

Bonny looked behind her. There on the shelf was a box labelled 'Number discs'. She handed it over. Cristalle disappeared, and Bonny turned up the microphones to hear what was happening.

In the far corner, Mrs Opalene was putting the final touches to Lulu's cowboy-sweetheart costume. Lulu was pouting at herself in the mirror.

'Look at me! I look *terrible*.'

'I think you look very nice, dear.'

'No, I don't! I've got bags under my eyes,

and skin so dry it's almost cracking.'

Mrs Opalene tilted Lulu's pretty gingham mob hat a tiny bit to the side. 'Does that look better?' She leaned over to inspect the pouting face in the mirror. 'Have you been going round without a sun hat, dear? I hope you haven't been forgetting the names of your dreaded Skin Enemies.'

'No, Mrs Opalene.'

'So you can tell me who they are?'

Lulu's answer came promptly enough. 'Sun. And Misery.'

'That's right, dear. And who are your precious Skin Helpers?'

'Sleep,' Lulu said dutifully. 'And Water. Lots of water.' Her face fell. 'I've forgotten the third one.'

Mrs Opalene looked pained.

'Oh, no, I haven't!' cried Lulu. 'It's Fresh Air!'

'Splendid!' declared Mrs Opalene. 'With plenty of sleep and water and fresh air, our skin can't go wrong!'

Ignoring Lulu's bad-tempered muttering – 'Well, *mine* has!' – Mrs Opalene sailed off to help Esmeralda with her ruffles. Bonny shook her head, mystified. Sleep. Water.

Fresh Air. All not just cheap, but *free*. How could Mrs Opalene be part of some fiendish plot to take people's money? Surely if that were true, then she'd be busy trying to persuade poor Lulu that what she needed was a costly pot of Glamour-Puss face cream, or an expensive tube of Skin-So-Soft. And now Bonny thought about it, even when Mrs Opalene had been going on earlier about face packs and elbow bleachers and stuff like that, she'd always saved her real enthusiasm for using up things like squeezed lemon halves, and old breakfast oatmeal.

No money in those. Anyone trying to help the glop men get rich quick would definitely have had the sense to say that only Rich-Girl-Bio-Face-Soothe-With-Added-Lano-Smarm-And-Derma-Tested-Gloss-Glaze (at twenty pounds a tub) would do the trick on Lulu's face.

And Mrs Opalene hadn't.

In fact, she'd said as many sensible as silly things. Keep off the fried foods. Eat fresh fruit and vegetables. Drink plain old water, not those sugary fizzy drinks. It might have been Bonny's mother talking. Toby was right. She must believe it all. The only problem was that she took it all so seriously. And so did they. It had become the only thing that mattered. It was the most important thing in their lives. Somehow, with all this fussing, they had forgotten how very rich and big and deep living could be. When Bonny thought about it, she realized that, all that morning, she'd never once heard any one of them turn to another and say, 'I missed you at swim club' (Wouldn't that muss up their hair!) or 'Are you coming camping this weekend?' (What scruffs they'd end up looking!) or even 'Meet you in the library on Saturday morning?' (Oh, no. They'd miss a whole four hours down the shops!)

No, Bonny thought glumly, watching them twirling and spinning and practising their prettiest faces. They were doomed. They had become like all those prissy milksops in the poems, walking in beauty but not going anywhere.

It was her job to save them, that was obvious.

But *how*? She couldn't go and talk to them because she was too busy with the sound and the lighting. And even those who weren't warming up were still frantically putting the last special touches to their make-up or their hair or their fancy costumes. They hadn't time to listen. And bossy Cristalle was already striding around with the box that she'd taken from Bonny's room.

'Time to choose places!'

One by one, each of them shut her eyes (carefully, so as not to smudge her make-up), whispered her own particular lucky chant, and picked out a coloured disc stamped with a number.

'Eight!' Cooki chortled. 'It's my lucky number!'

Lulu inspected her own disc. 'Five.' She groaned. 'Right in the middle. Who's going to remember anything you do if you're right in the middle?'

'One!' Serena's eyes shone with delight, though she said in pretend horror, 'Oh, it's *awful* going first. It's just horrible! Horrible!'

Cindy-Lou picked her number. 'Goody! I'm last! Everyone remembers the last one.'

One by one, each of them peeled the paper backing off their disc, and stuck the number on their music tape before bringing it to Bonny. They hadn't forgotten the incident with the pizza, she could tell. But no-one wanted to

♥134♥

get on the wrong side of her before the show, so they were all smiles and sweet voices.

'You will remember how I want my spotlight, won't you?'

'If I sing too softly, please turn down the backing tape.'

'My floodlights must stay on for the whole dance, you know.'

'Don't forget that my drum rolls get louder and louder.'

Bonny took notes, and put the tapes in order carefully. After all, if she was going to try and save them, it would be a whole lot easier if they liked and trusted her, and all that squabbling at the lunch table hadn't made the best start in that. So she was as friendly as she could be, nodding and smiling as they trooped in, and reassuring them when, terribly nervous, they explained what they wanted again, over and over.

And all the time Bonny was secretly hoping that Araminta would come in again, just to check about her lights and her snowflakes. This time, Bonny would get things right. First she would say how sorry she was the two of them had ended up quarrelling so horribly earlier. Then she'd apologize again, about the pizza. After that, she'd throw herself on Araminta's mercy, and beg her help in telling everyone how they were being used, and how they could be so much happier if they had other things to think about than just being pretty. Bonny worked it out in her mind. Araminta would sidle in, looking a little bit pouty and nervous. But once she was absolutely sure Bonny meant what she said, she'd listen carefully. When Bonny explained about the glop men, Araminta would look shocked, and say, 'Oh, let me help. We must explain to everyone. And now we're friends again, please call me Minty.'

So it was almost a surprise when Araminta pushed open the door and stood there, not halfway ready to be friends again, but scowling horribly.

Bonny stepped forward. 'I'm glad you've come. I was just going out to find you, to say I'm sorry.'

Araminta didn't smile.

'About the pizza? Or about being so mean to me earlier?'

Bonny was irritated, but she kept her temper.

'Mostly the pizza. After all, you were mean to me, too.'

'Not nearly as mean as you were.'

'Oh, please don't let's argue,' Bonny said. 'Shoving a pizza in someone's face may be worse than telling everyone that someone's jealous. But I said sorry first, and that's harder than anything.'

Araminta was still making a grumpy I'm-not-convinced face. The meeting really wasn't going as Bonny expected. But she pressed on, because it was important.

'But we have to be friends again, because I really need your help.'

'My help? Why?'

She looked so suspicious that Bonny knew it wouldn't work. Araminta wasn't going to listen. And, if she did, she wouldn't be convinced. And, if she were, she wouldn't help.

It was quite hopeless.

Or was it? In a flash, the idea came.

'Oh,' Bonny said innocently. 'I just had a little plan.'

'A little plan?'

'To please Mrs Opalene, so she'll forgive me for behaving so badly.'

'Please Mrs Opalene...?' Araminta's eyes lit up, as Bonny knew they would. Then she made a face, and said contemptuously, 'Now how would someone like you be able to please Mrs Opalene? It's impossible. She only has to look at you now, to get nervous. There's nothing you could do that would please her, except not cause any more trouble.'

'There is,' said Bonny. 'And I'm going to do it.'

Again, the glint shone in Araminta's eyes. 'What?'

'I wouldn't tell anyone else,' said Bonny. 'But I'll tell you. I'm going to brighten up the Curls and Purls Show.'

'Brighten it up?' Araminta looked doubtful. 'Why should—?'

'Listen,' interrupted Bonny. 'How many Curls and Purls shows have you been in, Araminta?'

'This is my seventh,' Araminta said.

'And how many do you think Mrs Opalene has judged?'

Araminta rolled her eyes upwards as she did the counting. 'Well, she's been running them since my half-sister went to Hooper Road School, and now she's getting on for twenty-two, and there are three a year, and so—' Araminta's eyes widened. 'She must have watched nearly fifty!'

'Exactly!' said Bonny. 'Fifty Curls and Purls shows. She must have seen every dance and heard every song a dozen times. I think she'd be delighted if someone fixed up something different. I bet she'd love a big surprise.'

Araminta was weakening, Bonny could tell. The Charm School girls would all do anything to please Mrs Opalene (especially on the day she chose the winner of the glistering tiara!). Bonny felt a bit bad about being so sneaky with someone who had come so close to being her friend, and whom she'd already upset by covering in pizza. But it was all in a good cause. The girls really should be saved from wasting any more of their lives.

So, leaning closer, Bonny whispered in Araminta's ear.

'Don't you think Mrs Opalene would be thrilled with someone who arranged a nice surprise for her? Something really *different*? Just for once? Don't you think she might even want to give them extra points?'

Araminta drew breath sharply. 'Extra points?'

'Not for me, obviously,' Bonny said casually. 'Because I'm not in the competition.'

'I am, though,' Araminta said, thinking fast.

'Oh, yes,' said Bonny. 'You are.' She shrugged so innocently. 'I suppose you might end up getting the extra points she would have given me, as well. Why, you might end up getting so many you walk off with the glistering tiara!'

She peeped slyly at Araminta, whose eyes were glinting with desire.

'The glistering tiara! Supreme Queen! Me! Oh, yes!' She spread her arms as if she were catching golden coins falling from heaven. 'Oh, yes! The glistering tiara! *Me!*'

Breaking off suddenly, she turned to Bonny. 'But how do I know I can trust you? You've never seemed to bother about Mrs Opalene having nice surprises before. Quite the opposite! You've given her several nasty ones. And me, too. So how do I know you're not just trying to get me into trouble? How do I know you don't want to win a crown of your own – the Spiteful Miss Sparky crown?'

Turning on Araminta that same, deeply reproachful, look that Mrs Opalene had given her earlier, Bonny put her hand on her heart and said in all honesty, 'I swear to you, Araminta. I'm doing this for the very, very best of reasons.'

Had she missed something? Did Mrs Opalene dish out marshmallow hearts along with the handy hints every Saturday morning? For suddenly Araminta was smiling happily from ear to ear. Reaching out to take Bonny's hands, she spun her round and round, just like before.

'Yes!' she said excitedly. 'Let's do it! Let's do it together! It'll be enormous fun. And we'll give darling, *darling* Mrs Opalene such a surprise!'

CHAPTER FIVE

Serena was first. Crossing her fingers for luck, she tripped up the steps onto the stage dressed in a frilly white Bo-Peep frock and carrying a crook garlanded with ribbons. Bonny wound the big handle labelled BACKDROP 1, and down behind Serena unfurled a painted farmyard scene, with crooked walls, and horses peering over stable doors. Serena wheeled a cardboard wishing well onto the stage. It had a bucket dangling from its winding bar and painted weeds growing up its side.

♥142♥

Serena turned her back to brush an invisible speck of dust from one of the frills on her frock.

Bonny seized the moment. 'Quick, Araminta!' she whispered through the only microphone still on SOUND OUT. 'Push the well over the trapdoor.'

Araminta dashed on the stage and pushed the cardboard well a few inches over. Then she glanced up at Bonny at the controls and put her thumbs up.

'Dear!' Mrs Opalene called. 'Shouldn't you be down here, in your seat?'

Araminta flashed Mrs Opalene one of her stunning, star-spangled smiles. 'I was just helping out a little,' she explained, 'because you've always said how very important it is to be as helpful as you can.' And she dashed off between the drapes into the wings, before Mrs Opalene could argue.

Serena turned back and gave the audience her prettiest smile. With her marking pencil in her hand, Mrs Opalene gave her a little wave.

'As soon as you're ready, dear ...'

Serena nodded at Bonny through the glass, and Bonny slid the first tape into the cassette player. After a moment's silence, in which Serena's set smile gradually began to freeze, out came a swell of violins, playing a sickly tune.

Serena sprang to life. Pressing the back of her hand against her forehead she began her song.

> '*My earring! My earring! I have lost it down the well.*
> *I reached over for the bucket, and into the depths it fell.*
> *Oh, what am I to do now? I am stricken! I am sad!*
> *For my earrings were a present from a handsome, charming lad.*'

At this point, Serena began to twirl, while heavenly choirs on the tape kept up the chorus without her.

> '*Her earring! Her earring! She has lost it down the well.*
> *Will her love survive this dreadful shock? Not one of us can tell.*'

Following Serena's instructions, Bonny turned up the drum rolls. Serena pressed her dainty fingertips to her temple and started on the second verse.

'If he peeps, he'll see it twinkle. If he peers, he'll see it flash.
And perhaps he will be angry, and away from me he'll dash.
He may fall in love with Flora from the farm along the way,
And I'll spend my whole life sobbing at the well-side. Lackaday!'

In the control room, Bonny whispered, 'Go!' Again, Araminta put her thumbs up, then, draping one of the fluffy white blankets they'd found in the storeroom tightly round her shoulders, she crept on all fours like a baby sheep, closer and closer to Serena, who was too busy twirling through the chorus to notice her.

Bonny's fingers were tingling with excitement over the switch labelled STAGE TRAPDOOR. As Serena embarked on the last verse, she waited for Araminta's little 'baa-aa' as a signal, then flicked it from CLOSED to

OPEN. Serena's song rang out quite loud enough to hide the low, mechanical rumble as the trapdoor slid open beneath the cardboard well.

'Since I know my love will leave me, and my tears I cannot quell,
In the darkness of despair and deepest misery I'll dwell.

In a dramatic gesture of grief, Serena raised herself on tiptoe and spread her arms. Just at that moment, Bonny pressed the two buttons labelled LIGHTNING FLASH and THUNDERCLAP, and Araminta the blanketed lambkin scuttled forward and butted Serena hard. Momentarily blinded by lightning, none of the audience saw. And deafened by thunder, none of them heard Serena's startled scream as, losing her balance totally, she dropped her beribboned crook and toppled out of sight into the well in a flurry of white bloomers.

But everyone heard the splash when she fell headfirst in the water bucket Bonny and Araminta had, giggling merrily, put underneath the trap door earlier.

Serena came up dripping just in time to hear the impostor sheep singing two new last lines to her song.

'And to maidens the world over the sad news this sheep will tell –
How she's gone to join her earrings at the bottom of the well!'

Everyone cheered. Some of them, it must be admitted, were just delighted because Serena looked so terrible, with ringlets like rats' tails and eyes smudged as black as coal holes. But all the others had very much enjoyed the song, with the excitement of the sheep creeping closer to Serena, the *flash!* and *bang!*, and the ungainly tumble down the well.

'Well done, Serena!'

'That was brilliant!'

Serena made a parting in her dripping hair, so she could peer out. Everyone was laughing and clapping. She stood a moment, wondering whether to giggle or cry. And then, deciding it would be a whole lot smarter to make the best of things, she spread her hands modestly.

'I just thought you'd all like something a little different,' she said. 'And it was *fun*.'

Everyone looked at Mrs Opalene, to see what she made of this change of plan. But, though she looked rather dubious, and anyone could tell she wasn't very much at ease with Serena's tangled wet hair and ruined make-up, she was still Mrs Opalene, and couldn't help saying something nice.

'Very—' She hesitated. 'Very *authentic*, dear!'

Not knowing what authentic meant, Serena took it for a compliment, and smiled very prettily all the way back down the stairs to her seat.

Araminta waved frantically at Bonny and pointed to the microphone.

Bonny switched to SOUND IN.

'You were right!' Araminta whispered excitedly. 'Mrs Opalene is *enjoying* it. She *did* want a change.'

She didn't have time to say more because Mrs Opalene was already calling, 'Next!'

Esmeralda was next. Smoothing her slinky green skirt, she took her place on the stage. In her bright yellow top, with matching petal hat, she looked exactly as she'd planned, like a willowy spring flower. Bonny flicked switches till the stage took on a sunlit hue. She wound down the backdrop Esmeralda wanted – another country scene – and dropped special effects sheets into the slots of the lanterns. Across the stage appeared a sprinkling of yellow dots, like a rash of spring flowers. And spinning across the painted blue sky were a host of puffy white clouds.

'The Buttercup Song,' declared Esmeralda. Waving her body from side to side, she started off.

'Gentle country breezes
Sway me to and fro,
Kiss me and caress me,
And make me lovely grow.'

In the control room, Bonny switched on a tape of sounds labelled 'Weather'. And, in the wings, Araminta turned the knob of Maura's wind machine on to BREEZE.

On the stage, Esmeralda's petal hat lifted and fluttered prettily. But on she sang.

'Lovely winds of heaven
Raise my petals high

To keep me ever busy
Worshipping the sky.'

Bonny forwarded the weather tape on to
'Very windy', and Araminta turned the wind
machine up a notch to match. Esmeralda
looked startled as her petals flapped violent-
ly. Clutching the rim of her hat, she raised
her voice above the gathering sound and
embarked on her third verse.

'Fearful storms of winter
Shall not come my way.
Safe and warm I stand here
On this mild spring day.'

Araminta winked at Bonny through a gap
in the side drapes and both of them, giggling,
turned up to STORM. One by one, all of
Esmeralda's petals tore from her hat and flew
off into the wings. Esmeralda was horrified.
But Mrs Opalene was still staring kindly, if a
little bemusedly, in her direction. And one of
the things she always said over and over was,
'The worst thing you can do on stage is stop.
Whatever happens, dears, press on. Press
on!'

So, bravely gripping the last remaining shreds of hat rim, Esmeralda sang on.

'What care I for tempests?
I shall have no fear.
A proud and yellow buttercup,
Simple flower of cheer.'

On the last note, Bonny and Araminta switched up to TEMPEST. Instantly both halves of Esmeralda's little buttercup outfit ripped off and swirled away into the wings. Determined not to fail at the last minute, Esmeralda resolutely bawled out the last verse in her vest and knickers.

'See me in my beauty!
Watch me in my pride!
A glorious golden buttercup,
Springtime's happy bride!'

Still grinning at one another, Bonny and Araminta switched to OFF. Just for a moment, Bonny feared there might have been some electrical fault because out in the big room the noise seemed to be carrying on without fading. But then she realized it was all the others, roaring their approval.

'Esmeralda, that was the funniest thing I've ever seen!'

'Brilliant!'

'You're so clever, keeping it a secret till the show!'

'You never told us you were so good at comedy skits!'

While they were all applauding, long and loud, Araminta rushed round the back of the stage and lifted Esmeralda's slinky green skirt off the lantern from which it was dangling. She ran on stage and handed it to Esmeralda, who hugged it to her body and proudly took bow after bow. Then, nervously, Esmeralda looked at Mrs Opalene.

Mrs Opalene's lips pursed. On the one hand, here was a girl with blown-about hair standing unashamedly on a stage in her underwear. But on the other hand, everyone was cheering frenziedly, and she did so want all of her girls to be happy.

'Well, dear,' said Mrs Opalene at last, choosing her words with care. 'That was a shade outlandish, I confess. But I think everyone enjoyed it thoroughly.'

Esmeralda beamed. She wasn't sure quite what outlandish meant. But she knew about enjoying things thoroughly. Especially warm applause. In fact, she wouldn't mind trying the song all over again sometime soon. She could do it even better. She could put in some of those silly faces she made to amuse her baby sister. And she could rewrite the words of the song so it was a weather forecaster standing there. That would be even funnier. Or she could—

'Next!' called Mrs Opalene firmly.

Amethyst floated up the steps onto the stage, flicked her hair and stood shyly in her glorious silver gown, cradling a glittering wand. She couldn't help feeling a little bit more nervous than usual. The other two had had such very exciting acts. They'd been such fun to watch. And all she had was ... Well, never mind. What Mrs Opalene always said was, 'Don't waste time wishing yourself like other people. Just make the best of what you have.'

What she had was pretty unexciting. But she'd make the very best of it.

'I'm going to perform *The Dance of the Evening Star*,' she explained to them carefully. 'I'm going to be Starlight. As evening falls around me, I wake and flutter to and fro, touching the wonders of nature lightly with my starry wand.' She waved it, to show them. 'And everything glistens with starlight, just for me, because everything loves me so much.'

In the control room Bonny shook her head in amazement that anyone would willingly dance something so soppy. She couldn't imagine anything more likely to banish any lingering doubts she might have had that she was doing Mrs Opalene's girls a giant favour, sparking up their Curls and Purls Show.

'Anyway,' went on Amethyst, 'I dance all night, except that, obviously, in the dance, the night only lasts two minutes. Then I curl up in my forest dell and fall asleep. And daybreak comes. Then I wake up and flee.'

'Lovely!' said Mrs Opalene, filled with relief that one of her precious girls, at least, was planning something more ladylike and traditional. 'Lovely, dear Amethyst! I do so look forward to seeing how very elegantly you can flee.'

Amethyst smiled. Her beautiful face lit up. 'Yes,' she admitted. 'I have been practising fleeing.' She turned to face the glass window and nodded at Bonny, who slid in music tape number 3, and wound down the forest backdrop Amethyst had chosen earlier.

Amethyst curled in a neat silver ball, and everyone waited. Out swelled the music. As its busy first bars gave way, within moments, to a more sleepy, going-to-bed sort of melody, the silver ball that was Amethyst gradually uncoiled a little, and the glittering wand waved gracefully in the air. Then she rose to her feet and looked around, making grand gestures of surprise and delight, as if she'd never seen an evening before.

And she'd certainly not seen one like this. It started well enough, with Bonny focusing exactly the right tree shadow shapes onto the stage, and turning the evening through the right shades of darkening blue while switching the stars up more brightly. Amethyst flitted round, flicking her hair prettily and pretending to pat each of the soppy, sloe-eyed creatures that were painted on the backdrop with her starry wand of evening.

'Aaaah!' everyone cooed dutifully when she tapped the baby deer sternly on its head.

'Ooooh!' everyone chorused politely when she shook her finger crossly at the chipmunks.

Amethyst swirled around, pretending to look for the squirrel.

And then she screamed. For from the branch over her head dangled the shadow of a massive spider. Amethyst skidded to an ungainly halt. In the control room, Bonny was jiggling the spider silhouette furiously in front of the lantern, and, on the stage, the spider shadow leaped obediently to the attack.

Amethyst screamed again. She'd secretly wanted something different. But this was horrible. Horrible! The whole stage darkened and the shadows loomed. Out went the stars, as if a cloud had swirled in front of them. Swampy green lights flickered eerily, and strange mists rose. In a frenzy of switch-flicking from Bonny, the baby deer ended up howling like a wolverine, the squirrel snarled, and when a demented chattering began to pour out of one of the loudspeakers behind the backdrop, Araminta suddenly had the bright idea of wheeling it behind the bit with the painted chipmunks, as if they'd suddenly come to life, and flown into a fury.

It was quite terrifying. From side to side ran Amethyst, desperate to find a way off the stage. She wasn't fleeing very elegantly, for all her hours of practice. Each time she thought she'd found a safe way to go, a shadow shaped like broken fingers seemed to snatch at her, or shadows of branches underfoot snaked out as if to trip her.

Her enthralled audience shouted.

'Try that way, Amethyst!'

'No! It's not safe! Try the other side!'

'Amethyst! Watch out!'

'Look behind you!'

Round and round Amethyst ran, in ever more desperate circles. From behind the backcloth came a werewolf's cry. And then another, sounding even closer.

Amethyst tore at her hair in fright. Sweat glistened on her face, melting her perfect make-up. Her lovely features twisted in terror and in the end she did the only thing that she could think of, and hurled herself back in a silver ball on the floor, covering her eyes with her fingers.

And that's when Bonny switched on the sounds of tiny, scurrying feet. Spreading her fingers slightly, Amethyst saw the little furry balls of shadow flitting across the stage.

'Oh, not rats! No!'

Amethyst jumped to her feet and started beating at them with her glittering wand. As the music came to an end and Bonny regretfully turned up the light to flood the stage with rosy dawn, Amethyst was to be seen clutching her torn skirts around her, still trying to beat to death a dozen skittering rats that were just shadows.

And how the audience clapped.

'Amethyst! Why didn't you tell us you could *act*?'

'My heart's still thumping, Amethyst. You ought to be in horror films! You're brilliant!'

'Do the scream again. Just one more time. It was so *bloodcurdling*.'

'I really thought that was a spider. And the rats fooled me too.'

'The rats fooled *everyone*. Did they fool you, Mrs Opalene?'

Mrs Opalene blinked hastily. It wouldn't do at all to admit that, ever since the spider, she'd had her eyes tightly closed. Not that it had helped much. She had still heard the werewolf's cry, the wolverine's snarl, and the terrified squeals from everyone around her.

Better say something, or they'd force her into watching it again, so she could mark it properly.

'Gratifyingly macabre, dear.'

Amethyst smiled bravely. She didn't know what gratifying meant. Or macabre, either. But now the lights were on again, she could at least get off the stage without falling over from fright. It hadn't been fun. It had been *terrifying*. But they were all talking about it so excitedly, and patting her on the back as she went shakily back to her seat. Only a minute ago, she could have cheerfully strangled that new Miss Sparky. Miss Electric Shock, more like! But now that her heart had stopped thumping, she could admit to herself that this *Dance of the Evening Star* must have been a whole lot more thrilling to watch than the usual old waking and fluttering and fleeing.

'Next!' called Mrs Opalene faintly.

Up on the stage walked Sarajane. But as Bonny reached for music tape number 4, she saw a shadow fall on the desk in front of her.

Hastily, she swung around.

'Toby!'

He nodded through the glass towards the stage. 'Brilliant!' he told her. 'Stunning! A real spectacular! It's quite amazing how much you've picked up in one short day.'

'Araminta's been helping. It turns out she knows a whole lot more than she ever realized. She's a real star at—'

He wasn't listening. He was looking worried.

'But you must promise me you won't make a fool of Sarajane.'

Bonny couldn't help staring. 'Oh, come on,' she managed to get out at last. 'If it's all right for the others, then it's all right for her. Sarajane is no different.'

'She is to me,' Toby said stubbornly. He blushed. 'I know that she can be as silly as all the others. But still I don't want her ending up head down in a well with her bloomers showing, or singing in her vest and knickers, or running round screaming.'

'Nothing wrong with that,' Bonny said, equally stubbornly. 'They're all enjoying it. You can tell.'

'It doesn't matter if she *does* it,' Toby said. 'It just matters that she gets to *choose*. And you haven't asked her.'

Bonny was silent. It was no more than the

truth. But they were halfway through the show now. She wasn't going to stop for anyone.

Bonny turned back to the controls. 'Sorry, Toby,' she said firmly. 'But I'm afraid Araminta and I are running this show.'

She felt a finger in the small of her back. 'Well, I'm afraid I'm warning you and your very good friend Araminta. Don't mess with Sarajane's song, or you'll regret it.'

Bonny made a face. So Cristalle was right. Toby was soft on Sarajane. But that was no reason for the two of them to change their plans. Araminta had already filled the bucket with water, and what could Toby do to them anyway? The day was very nearly over. How could a tea boy cause trouble for them? It was an empty threat. Of course he couldn't.

And then it struck her. Yes, he could. He could rush down and tell the lady on the desk what she and Araminta were doing, and she could hurry off to fetch Mum out of Bookkeeping (Advanced), and ...

Fetch Mum out of her class? Oh, that would be *awful*. It was so very near the end of the day that she might be in the middle of the test that would give her the certificate she needed so badly. Why, she might be on the very last question. To be so close, and have to lay down your pen and rush up to the third floor because of your troublesome daughter! What a way to start your new life in a brand new place.

'All right,' said Bonny sourly. 'You win.' But then suddenly, ringing in her ears again as if she'd somehow pressed the 'echo' switch, she heard the little phrase he'd used to warn her so sternly: 'you and your very good friend Araminta'.

And suddenly she didn't mind. Let Sarajane get on and do her bit in the Curls and Purls Show as soppily as she'd planned. If it mattered so much to Toby (and it obviously did), she'd just sit back and watch — with her good friend Araminta!

'All right,' she said again, a whole lot more cheerfully. 'We won't do anything to Sarajane. And that's a promise.'

CHAPTER SIX

Bonny slid in the music tape, and dropped into the revolving lantern the sheet that threw images of glittering rain. While Sarajane stood waiting for the excited chatter of the audience to die away, Bonny signalled frantically at Araminta to move to the nearest loudspeaker, then whispered. 'Don't throw the water!'

'Why not?' hissed back Araminta. 'It'll be *brilliant*. Everyone will love it.'

Already Sarajane was stepping forward.

'I can't explain,' Bonny whispered hastily.

'There isn't time. But just don't throw it. Don't do *anything*. Promise?'

Araminta shrugged, disappointed. But, like a good friend, she answered trustingly, 'Well, if you say so.'

Sarajane was explaining now. 'This is a lovely little song and dance called *Pretty Miss Raindrop*. It starts with a great peal of thunder so you mustn't be startled. And then I fall to earth in a glittering shower. There aren't many words in the song.' She stopped, embarrassed. 'Well, actually, the only words in it are *'Drip, drip, drip'*. But I do sing them over and over.'

More of a threat than a promise, Bonny thought privately. But she obediently pressed PLAY when Sarajane gave the signal. There was a moment's silence. Then, from the speakers, flowed the plaintive sound of violins.

Bonny waited for the thunderpeal. (Sarajane had told her three times over that this was the cue to switch on the glittering shower.) But nothing like a peal of thunder came, only the music rising and falling like souls lost in grief. Bonny peeked through the glass. Poor Sarajane looked positively stricken. Could this be the wrong music? She glanced at the empty tape box. Yes, it was number 4. But in the rush to speak to Araminta after Toby's warning, might she have slid it in on the wrong side?

Oh, no! Toby would kill her when he realized there was something wrong. In desperate hope, Bonny held on for one or two more bars, in case the thunder came. But it was hopeless. It didn't sound at all the right sort of music for rushing round being a raindrop. Clearly the only thing to do was take out the tape and start again. Sarajane looked more and more panicked as the wrong music poured out behind her. And a great scowl was gathering on Toby's face.

Bonny's finger reached out for the STOP button. But just at that moment, Sarajane threw back her head and opened her mouth wide. Bonny hesitated. Had she decided to press on and sing whatever it was she had recorded on the other side?

The haunting melody rose. And out of Sarajane's mouth there poured a waterfall of notes so pure and lovely that Bonny's hand froze from sheer enchantment.

'Dark my days, and dark my hours
Since Lord Henry broke my heart.
I'll forsake these golden bowers
And the seas of grief I'll chart.'

Beside her, Toby moved closer to the glass.
Already the glower on his face had cleared.
He looked entranced, and Bonny could see
the fingers on his left hand twitching, as
though, as he listened, he was playing the
melody along with his precious Sarajane on
some imaginary violin.

The glorious voice poured out of the loudspeakers. Even Araminta had put down the
bucket and stopped looking wistful as she
listened.

'Lost my hopes, and lost my beauty
Since Lord Henry rode away.
Was there ever such a cruelty?
Was there ever such dismay?'

The lovely voice soared. Even if Toby
weren't in the way, rapt and unreachable,
there was no need for Bonny to switch on any
glittering showers. Sarajane's voice alone

could glitter and sparkle, flash and blaze. All Bonny had to do was keep the simple spotlight trained on her. If she could sing like this and steal their hearts, why should she bother even to step out of the bright circle of light that was all Bonny offered?

'Will Lord Henry hear my singing?
Shall I charm him back to me,
In his ears, my verses ringing,
In his heart, my melody?'

The music swelled and died. The song was over. Sarajane hung her head, deeply embarrassed, and, for a moment or two, there was no sound at all.

Beside Bonny, Toby stirred uneasily. Beyond the glass, the clapping started. Araminta put the bucket back where it was supposed to be, and Mrs Opalene dabbed at her eyes with a frilly lace handkerchief.

Toby's eyes shifted to the audience. 'Whose is that spare seat next to Sarajane's?'

'It's Araminta's. She's not using it.'

Instantly, he was at the door. 'Silly to waste it.'

'You're soft on Sarajane, aren't you?'

Did he even hear her? She didn't think so. He'd already gone. Bonny sighed heavily. And after all those lofty speeches about silly girls! (Though, to be fair, he'd stuck with just feeling soft until he'd heard her singing so beautifully. It was her talent, not her pretty face, that had bewitched his heart.)

As he slipped into Araminta's empty seat, Mrs Opalene rose from her own overfull one.

'My dearest Sarajane,' she said, still plainly moved. 'That was *incomparable.*'

Nobody knew what incomparable meant. But it was obvious it was a compliment of the highest order, so everyone happily nodded along. And, after that, it was quite clear to them that Mrs Opalene was almost as taken with the new-style Curls and Purls Show as her pupils.

'Memorable, dear! Memorable!' she said, enchanted, after Lulu's 'cowboy sweetheart' song, when Araminta popped up behind the cardboard stockade wearing the bison horns she'd found in the stockroom, and Bonny turned on the tornado and sent tumbleweed bouncing across the prairie backdrop.

'Exotic!' she marvelled after the firework explosions that shook the stage all through Cristalle's lullaby.

'Rivetingly tasteless, dear,' was her judgement after Angelica's *Beauty and her Mirror* song, during which Bonny fiddled with the lighting until Angelica aged horribly before their eyes, then turned into a skull.

'Disquietingly vertiginous,' she said faintly when Araminta's own turn finally came round, and Bonny made the snowflakes swirl so fast that Araminta finally got dizzy and fell over.

And how Bonny managed to turn Cooki's pretty fairy ring of mushrooms into that waterlogged swamp of crocodiles, Mrs Opalene swore she'd never know.

At last it was over. Cindy-Lou swatted out fiercely one last time at all the shadow bats that had so mysteriously swooped in to join her gracious *Tea-time with the Vicar* mime. Down came the curtain, and Mrs Opalene sailed up the stairs and stood on the stage apron.

'Well, dears!' she declared. 'That was ...'

And, for the first time in her life, Mrs Opalene was lost for words.

'Such *fun*,' said Araminta, coming out of the wings, and hugging Mrs Opalene. 'Such wonderful fun!'

'Marvellous!' called out Lulu.

'Fabulous!'

'Terrific!'

Pearl hugged herself. 'It was,' she breathed in ecstasy, 'the very best Curls and Purls Show *ever*!'

Mrs Opalene capitulated graciously. 'Yes, dears. I do agree it made the most amusing and interesting change. And we must certainly think of doing it that way again some other time.'

'Not just some other time, Mrs Opalene! *Next* time!'

'Not just *next* time, Mrs Opalene! *Every* time!'

Mrs Opalene looked down at them, startled. Where were the modest and amenable girls with whom she'd spent the morning? Sitting in front of her now were a crowd of smudged, untidy urchins, fidgeting and grinning, and calling out, uncurbed.

'Now, girls!' she reproved them. 'Aren't we beginning to forget that we try to stay very best friends with Miss Manners?'

At the words, 'very best friends', Araminta swivelled in her seat and blew a sparkling, Araminta-ish kiss at Bonny through the glass.

Bonny had never blown a kiss before. Like lots of other things in Charm School that day, it was a first. She blew it back while Mrs Opalene went on with her lecture. 'In fact, dears, as you know, ladies *never* shout out like this when they want something. They simply think of a roundabout way of suggesting it nicely, in the hope that—'

But no-one was listening.

'Mrs Opalene!' Pearl's voice rose over the

others. 'That was such fun that I don't think I could go back to doing it the old way. There was just too much sitting around and waiting. And watching everyone else mince up and down looking pretty was boring too.' She sighed wistfully. 'I had such *fun* today. Amethyst was *brilliant*. I wish I could act like that.' Suddenly, a thought struck her. 'Do they do acting classes here, as well?'

Some of those listening couldn't help noticing there was a shade of bitterness in Bonny's voice as it came through the loudspeaker. 'Yes, there are acting classes, but they don't start till next week.'

Once again, Mrs Opalene found herself facing unladylike chaos.

'Acting!'

'Yes!'

'Oh, I'd *adore* to learn to act!'

'And are there painting classes, too? If there were, I'd go to them. Then I could paint Amethyst an even *creepier* forest backdrop.'

'Saturdays,' Bonny informed Suki. 'Two till four. Bring your own paints.'

'Sarajane should take singing. Or choir. If I had a voice as lovely as hers, I wouldn't want to waste it.'

'Tuesdays, at six.'

'I've always wanted to learn juggling, personally.'

'Thursdays, from January till April.'

'Did you see the tornado? And the prairie? And the swamp full of crocodiles? I'd love to know more about those sorts of things.'

'Natural geography,' Bonny informed her through the loudspeakers. 'On Wednesdays at lunchtime, repeated Friday nights.'

Mrs Opalene saw her class melting away before her eyes.

'Girls! Girls!' she said. 'Perhaps Pearl's right. Maybe it would be nice to—' she wondered how to put it '—*broaden out* a little.'

'What? Learn a few other things? Like how to work the lights, and the sound?'

'And make people laugh?'

'And tell jokes?'

'And juggle!'

'Excellent! In that case, I'll certainly be coming back.'

'Me, too!'

'And me.'

Mrs Opalene looked thrilled. 'Really, dears? Oh, I'm so pleased. And maybe, over time, we'll get to find extra things to interest *everyone*.'

A dreamy look spread over Cooki's face. 'I'll tell you what interested me. Those astonishing fireworks. They were *breathtaking*!'

'*My* breath,' Cristalle reminded her. 'I was so terrified, I could hardly finish my lullaby.'

'Oh, but they looked so *real*. I *loved* them.' The dreamy look sharpened. 'Do you suppose that we could broaden out enough to learn how to make fireworks, Mrs Opalene?'

Mrs Opalene blanched. 'No, dear. I don't think so. I fear, if we took up with flashes and explosions, we'd end up stepping on Dr Hooper's toes.'

'Who's Dr Hooper?'

'Chemistry,' Bonny informed them. 'Tuesdays, at five.' She couldn't help adding, with the tinge of bitterness they'd all come to recognize, 'But that's another class that doesn't start till September.'

'That's fine. I'll wait,' said Cooki. 'Do you want to come with me, Angelica?'

'No.' Angelica was adamant. 'I'm definitely off to do Geography.'

How odd, thought Bonny, still in the control room. Only this morning they'd have been wishing one another away sick in bed, or off on holiday, so there'd be fewer of them out to win the glistering tiara. Now they were asking one another to come along to these new classes – even the ones who hadn't seemed good friends before.

'Lulu? Will you come?'

Lulu was torn. 'The fireworks were lovely. But, no. I'm still going to choose painting.'

Mrs Opalene looked crestfallen. Suki consoled her. 'Never mind. You mustn't worry. You'll still have plenty of people. Because, now we won't just be walking in boring old beauty all the time, a lot of our friends will probably start coming too.'

Mrs Opalene clasped her hands eagerly. 'Oh, do you think so?'

'I'm sure so. Now that we won't be spending all our time suffering to be beautiful.'

Cooki looked up. 'If we don't have to suffer to get in those frocks all the time, then I'll come back to Charm School as well as Chemistry.' Under her breath, she added mischievously, 'And I'll have two slices of pizza, if I'm hungry!'

'I'll carry on coming as well!'

'Me, too!'

'And me!'

Mrs Opalene cheered up. 'Well, dears,' she

said. 'Perhaps it's all for the best. I have been giving these classes for years and years. And times do change. If you're all busy doing all these other interesting things, you simply won't have quite so much time to sit with your elbows in lemon halves, and wander round the shops looking for just the right thing.'

Her eye fell on Toby, holding Sarajane's hand.

'Though I do hope, whatever you're all busy doing, you'll always try and remember how to *behave*.'

A thought struck Araminta suddenly.

'Won't we have to change the Charm School motto, now we won't be suffering any more?'

Mrs Opalene looked anxious. 'Oh, dear! Oh, dear!'

'I know!' cried Lulu. 'How about, *Handsome is as Handsome does?*'

'What about, *Beauty is in the eye of the Beholder?*' called out Esmeralda.

'I quite like, *Beauty is Truth, Truth Beauty*,' quoted Cooki.

Horrified, Mrs Opalene put up her hand to stem the rising tide of heresy. 'Shall we leave that till later, dears? For the moment, let's just decide who we're going to crown the Supreme Queen, and then we'll do all these other things next time.'

Next time! Bonny looked round at the chaos in the control room and wondered what on earth the famous Maura would think of all the mess when she came back. Leaping off her swivel chair, she hastily started putting things away in boxes. She didn't want Maura complaining to Mrs Opalene. Mrs Opalene might not be keen to have her back.

And she might want to come. After all, if Charm School was, as she hoped, about to turn into Fun School, it would be a wonderful way of spending time with Araminta. Though they might even turn out to be in the same school... In the same class, even! Thinking how wonderful this would be, Bonny stuffed one slide and stencil and cassette after another into what she hoped were the right places. She was still busy putting things away when Araminta burst in.

'Ah!' Bonny joked. 'Just the person I need. Miss Tidy by Nature!'

But Araminta wasn't listening. Rushing to a little cabinet on the wall, she unlocked it, and carefully drew out a beautiful sparkling tiara set on a flat satin cushion spangled with shimmering crystal beads.

Holding it reverently, she walked past Bonny, busy on her knees, and carried it back to Mrs Opalene.

Mrs Opalene held it high.

'I wish there was one for everybody,' she said. 'You all gave such fine performances. It's so hard to decide. And we never even got round to doing the catwalk parade, which might have helped me choose the winner properly.'

'We could still do that now,' suggested Angelica.

Mrs Opalene looked down at them all, and shuddered. 'I don't think so, dears. You all look a little bit—' the word was 'scruffy', but it seemed so rude '—*unpolished*. And I'm afraid I somehow mislaid my marking pad while that frightful wolverine was growling at Amethyst. So, dears, I'm horribly afraid I'm not quite sure who ought to be—'

But Araminta was on her feet again in her excitement.

'It's obvious, Mrs Opalene! There's someone here who's won it fair and square. Amethyst made us scream with terror, stuck in that awful forest. And Serena made us laugh ourselves silly, tumbling into that well. And Sarajane made us cry with her beautiful singing.' In the interests of honesty, she amended this. 'Well, *some* of us,' she added politely. 'But who made all of us do it?'

They were silent. In their heart of hearts, every single one of them knew that, but for one person, at this very moment they'd have been mincing up and down the catwalk in their pretty frocks, trying to look beautiful enough to win the glistering tiara. And instead of bouncing up and down excitedly on their seats, as they were now, making interesting plans for the future, all except one of them would have gone home and sobbed into her pillows, feeling nothing but clumsy, or podgy, or ugly.

It was a struggle. But they'd had a brilliant afternoon. And there were good times to come.

'All right. That's fair enough.'

'Yes. I agree.'

'She did a *spectacular* show.'

'Those bats!'

'Those *rats*!'

'Personally, I loved the tumbleweed. Do you suppose I should be thinking of classes in Botany?'

Deep in her boxes, Bonny overheard the word 'Botany' coming through the sound system. 'Mondays,' she called out automatically. 'Between six and eight, with optional Saturday field trips.'

Once again, Mrs Opalene had visions of a vanishing class.

'Right, then,' she said hastily. 'Since you obviously all agree, the glistering tiara goes to—'

Everyone shouted it together.

'Miss Sparky!'

Startled, Bonny looked up from her tidying.

'What?'

'Miss Sparky!' Mrs Opalene called out again. 'Our own Supreme Queen! Time to be crowned, dear, with our lovely glistering tiara.'

All the blood drained from Bonny's face.

'Oh, no! Oh, no!'

Staying on all fours, she made for the door. The knees of her jeans picked up huge dusty smudges, but she didn't care. She just kept her head down and carried on scuttling towards the huge green glowing sign that promised EXIT.

Two leggy pillars suddenly barred her way. Toby.

'And where do you think you're going?'

'Home!' Bonny whispered. 'Quickly! Before they get me!'

'They're not planning on *hanging* you,' Toby pointed out. 'They simply want to make you Supreme Queen.'

'Well, it's *ridiculous*.'

'No, it isn't.'

'Yes, it is!'

'Well,' Toby said judiciously. 'I do agree it is a *little* strange that you should be the winner.' A soppy smile spread over his face. 'I mean, it is a bit difficult to see how anyone could have chosen you after that touching and heart-rending song about Lord Henry—'

'Excuse *me*,' Bonny interrupted tartly. 'But if it weren't for me, your precious Sarajane would have sung a song that goes, "Drip, drip, drip".'

'But that was just your mistake.'

He was quite right, of course. But he'd annoyed her. For a moment she couldn't think of any suitable retort. And then Mrs Opalene's words came back to her, about reaching the heights of fashion. And she told him loftily, 'On the contrary. It was a combination of vision, and planning, and hard, hard work.'

He looked impressed. 'Oh, well,' he said. 'In that case, fair enough. After all, Sarajane probably has a whole lifetime of singing prizes in front of her.' He blushed. 'In fact, she says she's going to let me accompany her on my violin. So, now I *really* need a better one, I won't mind doing this boring job so much each Saturday.'

'If Mrs Opalene's classes go the way I think they're going,' Bonny said, 'your job won't be so boring in future.'

'True.' He looked delighted. 'Well, then,' he said. 'You seem to have sorted out just about everybody in one short day. I definitely think that you deserve the glistering tiara.'

Bonny thought about it for a moment. She looked at all the lamps and equipment she'd worked so hard to learn how to handle, so they could have their brilliant show. And she thought of the changes she'd made for them. And she thought of Araminta.

'Yes,' she agreed. 'I think that I deserve it, too. I've earned it fair and square. I'll wear it with pride.'

'Good,' Toby said. 'And Sarajane can be crowned with my admiration instead.'

'That's nice,' said Bonny. 'She'll look good in that.' And, laughing, she walked out as Toby opened the door for her, bowing like a footman.

Everyone was waiting. Mrs Opalene beamed. 'Ah, there you are, dear! It is a pity we don't have time to dress you up a bit, just for the presentation. You would have looked such a treat in Cindy-Lou's Blushing Rose frock. But, never mind. We must just make the best of things.'

Obligingly, Bonny dusted the knees of her jeans before walking up the steps.

Mrs Opalene held the glistering tiara aloft. Its rhinestones sparkled and the sequins sewn onto its velvet rim twinkled in the gleam of the one spotlight Bonny hadn't yet switched off.

'It gives me *inordinate* pleasure,' said Mrs

Opalene, 'to place this precious crowning glory onto the head of our most deserving Supreme Queen: *Miss Sparky!*'

None of them knew what inordinate meant. But they cheered anyway as Mrs Opalene wedged the tiara firmly on the unruly hedge of Bonny's hair, and Cindy-Lou took a photo.

'There, dear! Don't you look nice?'

Bonny could see from her reflection in every mirror round the room that hers would be the first of all the photographs in the corridor outside to show a grimy face with unbrushed hair wearing the prized tiara.

Her look of triumph, though, would fit in very well.

'Thank you,' she told them all. 'Thank you. I've had a wonderful day. I can't remember when I last had so much fun. I'm really glad I chose to come to Charm School.'

'Are you, dear?'

Mrs Opalene was *thrilled*.

Bonny couldn't help hugging her. 'Yes. Yes, I am. And I'll be back again next time, if you'll let me.'

'My dear, we'll be honoured,' Mrs Opalene said. 'Honoured and *charmed*.'

The rest of the afternoon passed in a flash of tidying, and laughing, and swapping jokes and stories, and putting away chairs, and exchanging phone numbers and addresses. It seemed to Bonny it was half an hour at most before Mrs Opalene finally ushered the last of them out into the corridor and along to the lift.

'Bye, dears! Take good care! See you all next time!'

'Bye, Mrs Opalene! Bye!'

On the ground floor, Bonny spilled out of the lift, giggling, surrounded by chattering girls. Beside the desk, Mrs Bramble stood holding her certificate, and talking to the lady who had sold them their tickets. Both of them stared as Bonny rushed over to greet them.

Neither could understand how that sour and resentful creature from whom they'd parted that morning could have turned into the bubbling, excited person in front of them now.

'Mum! Mum! Come and meet Minty!' She pointed round the group of girls. 'And Cooki! And Lulu! And Esmeralda! And Cindy-Lou! And—'

Mrs Bramble waved her certificate in Bonny's face. Snatching it, Bonny inspected her mother's name on the dotted line, then hugged her proudly. 'You did it! Brilliant! Well done!'

'What about you?' asked Mrs Bramble. And then, unable to deny the evidence of Bonny's shining eyes, and all the girls gathering round her, she risked the tiniest little tease.

'A little bit better than you expected, was it?'

Bonny's face was radiant. 'Better? It was *brilliant*! I learned so much, and made so many friends. I even won their funny old glistering tiara, and I'm Miss Sparky for a whole year! And Minty's going to phone me tonight – if the phone's on yet. And, Mum, can I come back again next time Mrs Opalene runs

Charm School? Oh, please, please, *please*! I'll help unpack all the packing crates, and sort out the plates and dishes, and put things away in cupboards, and—'

She reached for her mother's basket.

'Oh, let me carry all those heavy accounting books. You must be tired. I'll take these to the car.'

Mrs Bramble stared at her daughter. What on earth had happened all day up there on the third floor? What on earth was the glistering tiara? How would you get to be a Miss Sparky? And who was this Mrs Opalene, who'd weaved such magic over the miserable, sullen daughter she'd been arguing with that morning?

No time to ask now. Already Bonny was frantically waving and calling to a couple leaving arm in arm. 'Bye, Toby! Bye, Sarajane!' In fact, she didn't stop waving and calling out her merry goodbyes to her new friends till they were safely in the car.

Mrs Bramble could hardly believe it.

Only one day at Charm School.

But it worked.

Miss Sparky

ABOUT THE AUTHOR

ANNE FINE was born in Leicester. She went to
Wallisdean County Primary School in Fareham,
Hampshire, and then to Northampton High School for
Girls. She read Politics and History at the University of
Warwick and then worked as an Information Officer for
Oxfam before teaching (very briefly!) in a Scottish
prison. She started her first book during a blizzard that
stopped her getting to Edinburgh City Library and has
been writing ever since.

Anne Fine is a hugely popular and celebrated author.
Amongst the many awards she has won are the
Carnegie Medal (twice), the Whitbread Children's Novel
Award (twice), the Guardian Children's Literature
Award, a Smarties Prize, and she has twice been voted
Children's Writer of the Year.

She has written over forty books for children and adults,
including *Goggle Eyes*, *Flour Babies*, *Bill's New Frock*,
The Tulip Touch and *Madame Doubtfire* (which was
made into a feature film by Twentieth Century Fox,
starring Robin Williams).

Charm School was Anne Fine's first novel for
Doubleday/Corgi Yearling Books. A second title, *Bad
Dreams*, is also published by Doubleday.

www.annefine.co.uk
